GOTTA LET IT GO

Copyright © 2010 by Deliah Lawrence.

Second Edition 2017.

Library of Congress Control Number: 2010909950
ISBN 978-0-9981032-0-4

This is a work of fiction. Names, characters, places and incidents either are the product of the author's imagination or are used fictitiously, and any resemblance to any actual persons, living or dead, events, or locales is entirely coincidental.

This book was printed in the United States of America.

Interior Format

GOTTA LET IT GO

DELIAH LAWRENCE

ACKNOWLEDGMENTS

A S ANY PUBLISHED AUTHOR OR non-published writer would agree, writing is not an easy task. While I enjoyed writing *Gotta Let It Go*, I wouldn't have been able to complete it without the love, support, and encouragement from my family and friends, so I'd like to give special thanks to:

God, through Him all things are possible and I truly believe that.

N. Henlon, my mother and C. Cruickshank, my brother. You're both my rock and my inspiration. Thanks for encouraging me to fulfill my passion as a writer. I love you both.

The Talented Scribes (my writers' critique group): M. Paris, L. Trovillion, T. Waters, and S. Yanguas. They are a highly spirited and supportive group of writers of fantasy, young adult, mystery, and coming of age novels. Thanks for all your insights, suggestions, and comments in shaping up GLIG.

L. Lough, a fellow writer, and creative writing instructor. Thanks for encouraging me to find my own unique voice and to never give up on the idea of seeing my words in print.

A. Chapman, my gym buddy, sister from another mister, and my editor. Thanks for sharing your suggestions and ideas over wings and cocktails at Houlihan's and P.F. Chang's. You're the best!

C. Cruickshank, thank you for a second pair of eyes and your fresh perspective. Your contribution was invaluable.

L.S. Ferguson and L. Collins, my friends who read the first draft of GLIG. Thanks for your suggestions and positive feedback.

L.Z. Ringgold, my law school buddy. Thanks for answering my many questions regarding police procedures.

To all the readers everywhere; thanks for your love and support.

It would be great to hear from you, so please e-mail me at dlawmba@gmail.com.

ALSO BY
DELIAH LAWRENCE

GOTTA GET IT BACK
(Coming Soon)

ANTHOLOGIES

Creatures, Crimes and Creativity
Lucky Tuesday – 2013
Georgia Peach – 2014

CHAPTER 1

A NOTHER RESTLESS NIGHT. I COULD hear the rustling of the crisp autumn leaves outside my windows as I tossed and turned under my comforter. I knew I had to get up, but I pulled the covers over my head and snuggled deeper into the sheets instead. Today was going to be a turning point in my life and I can either face it like the strong sister that I am or do the fake out and cancel the meeting.

"Just like the Calgon commercial, I really gotta get up outta here and go somewhere." The lyrics from Mariah Carey's song "Shake It Off" came blaring from my clock radio set to WPGC-FM (95.5).

"Brrrrr, gee thanks, Mariah. Damn, I guess that's my cue to get up." I sat on the edge of my bed, yawned, outstretched my arms and stepped into my fluffy pink slippers. I showered and then dried off as I was walking toward my bed. I got dressed in my black Donna Karan pantsuit and finished my look with some pearl earrings and necklace. I did the once over in my mirror, making sure that my flat ironed shoulder length hair was perfect and my cinnamon complexion was flawless. I smiled and was pleased that I would make his head turn just once more.

I was moving slower than usual, but thank God I had set the coffee to perk the night before to save some time. I always loved smelling the aroma from the coffee but this morning it made me queasy, forcing me to eat a half tube of Tums. I filled my travel mug with hot coffee, grabbed my car keys and then set the alarm system before heading to the meeting. As I locked the front door, I saw my next door neighbor, Larry, doing his daily chore of washing his red Chrysler Crossfire sports car.

"Morning, Larry," I said, waving to him.

"Morning neighbor! Sure is brisk out here today," he said, grinning as he polished the car's chrome rims.

I wanted to ask why he was polishing the car again, when he had done it only yesterday. "Sure is," I said instead. Men.

In my silver Audi sedan, not even the sound of Prince's "Musicology," could help me get over the dreaded drive to the Law Offices of Hardwick and Knox, nestled in the heart of Baltimore's Inner Harbor.

Traffic on I-95 was surprisingly smooth for a Friday morning, and when I arrived at Hardwick's office, I slid into the last available space in front of the building. My hands were shaking as I checked my watch. 8:15 a.m., I noted. The bright morning sun glinted from the tall windows of the newly renovated warehouse, and I squinted. As if the building wasn't intimidating enough, I needed to gather my strength just to hit the UP button on the elevator. Once I reached the fourteenth floor, I'd start the process of bidding my seven year marriage a final farewell. Hopefully, then I could recapture what little was left of me.

The elevator doors hissed open, exposing burgundy carpet, rustic brick walls with bold brass letters that spelled out the firm's name, and big photos of the founding partners hanging in mahogany frames. Nice layout, I thought, impressed despite myself.

I inhaled deeply, straightened the sides of my jacket, stood tall and lifted my chin, then marched up to the receptionist's desk.

"Good morning," I said. "I have an 8:30 appointment with Mr. Hardwick."

The freckle-faced assistant peered over her brown square-rimmed glasses. "Please have a seat, Mr. Hardwick will be with you shortly," she said, hesitating as if unsure whether to notify Hardwick or tell me to take a hike. "Would you care for some coffee, tea, or juice while you wait?"

"No thanks," I said, putting my handbag on the table beside one of several green velvet chairs. I sat, then leaned toward the magazine rack and withdrew a *Jet* magazine. How sad, I thought, staring at the full-color likeness of Bernie Mac, gone too soon and missed by many adoring fans. I thumbed through the issue, hoping to find more pictures paying tribute to the "King of Comedy."

"Hmm, hmm, hmm. Good morning, Deidre."

Just hearing his voice so soft and smooth made me quiver. "G'morning, Kyle," I said without looking up. Though he stood three feet away, I could smell the crisp manly scent of *Gucci Rush*, I was about to tell him he should consider going a little easy on the stuff when he gently placed a hand on my shoulder.

Instantly, shivers shot down my spine and my nipples stood at attention. I closed the magazine, knowing when I signed those papers in a few minutes; I'd be closing the chance of ever finding a man who'd have such an impact on me, physically and emotionally.

I sighed and returned the *Jet* to its proper slot in the rack. I needed that bit of time to compose myself and rein in my determination. Only then could I look up into those deep brown eyes. I wasn't surprised when he flashed that come-hither smile or shrugged one broad shoulder as if he knew better than I the way he affected me.

But this tall, bedroom-voiced sex machine was about to become my ex-husband.

The glint in his eyes dimmed, and his smile faded when I got to my feet. "So," he said, clasping his hands behind his back. "I guess, this is it, huh?"

He looked at me with sad puppy eyes which always softened my heart and made me forgive him his indiscretions over and over again. But not this time. As I remembered his words, "you'll never win," which he spat at me like venom when he received the divorce papers, and they jolted me back to reality. Without a doubt, I had to go through with this, right here and right now.

"Yup," I said, gritting my teeth. He had a real talent for rattling me. Every time I caught him lying or cheating, he somehow managed to turn things in his favor by focusing on 'extenuating circumstances,' or 'the entertainment'—his definition of the women he bedded. I loved him, but it was no ordinary love. It was the type of love that would make me go crazy or would kill me slowly. And I loved me.

He nonchalantly stretched out one arm, then the other, to adjust his gem studded cufflinks in the sleeves of his starched white shirt. "So where's your attorney?" he asked, smoothing the blue silk tie that matched the pinstripes of his elegant Italian suit.

I couldn't sit down any longer and let him continue to have the upper hand. So I straightened my back and then stood up next to him. Despite being five-seven from wearing three inch heels, he stood almost six inches taller than I, and he overshadowed me.

"Not to worry," I snapped, grabbing my handbag. "We don't want to keep you from being single a minute longer than necessary." I tucked my handbag under my arm so hard I thought surely I would find a bruise later. "You've always been single in your mind and heart...and married only when it served your purpose."

I looked down the long hallway, wondering which office belonged to Hardwick, because I wanted nothing more than to high-tail it in there, sign the damned papers, and be on my way.

"Aw, Deidre," he said, aiming that brilliant smile my way. "Don't be like that." And like a father gently scolding his errant daughter, he added, "You always knew I needed more, that I liked living on the edge...but *you're* the only one I ever really loved...the one I'll always love."

I prayed to God he hadn't seen me cringe. Prayed he wouldn't see the tears that stung my eyes, either. That voice, smooth as satin, had been my undoing too many times to count. Because he was right, damn him, I *had* known it, and the knowledge created an ache deep inside me that would likely never fade. Worse still, I loved him, and that would likely never fade, either.

Just as I was about to respond, he thumped the heel of his hand against his forehead. Winking, he headed toward the elevator. "Be back in a flash...left my briefcase in the car. Don't let 'em start without me."

I watched Kyle disappear into the elevator, averting my eyes as the doors hissed shut. Damn the sexy, confident, successful man! Damn the way he could charm the pants off any woman regardless of her race, color or creed!

"Smooth Operator," I muttered, pacing the space between the elevator and the receptionist's desk, hoping my lawyer would arrive before Kyle returned.

Where was she, anyway? I reached into my handbag to get my cell phone when it began vibrating, startling me so badly I nearly dropped it.

One glance at the caller ID told me it was my tardy lawyer. "Hello."

I met the receptionist's eyes as I walked toward the open conference room, pointing to let her know I'd take the call in there, and she nodded.

"Deidre, it's Lia. Sorry I'm late but traffic was *all* backed up on 95. I'm pulling into the parking lot now. Explain and apologize for me...but don't discuss anything with anyone until I get there. Hear?"

"Girl, you don't know how glad I am you're finally here." If Kyle returned and layered more of his suave sophistication on me, I'd walk out of here just as married as when I walked in. "Hurry up now, 'cause I really need to go through this settlement conference before I change my mind about getting rid of that...that *man*."

The word was like magic, summoning the image of him in his dark suit...I shook my head. "You can probably see him by now, coming out of the building. He said he left his briefcase in his car, but you know how he lies. He's probably got his cell phone pressed to his ear, setting up a fuck date to celebrate his freedom," I laughed, but didn't mean it.

"Nope," Lia said. "Can't see him...yet, anyway."

"We'll talk more when you get up here. Now hurry, girl, will you!"

I was about to hang up when Lia chuckled. "Well, well, well... here comes Mr. GQ now, and just like you predicted, his cell phone's stuck to his ear," she paused, then added, "Mmm-hmm that's a purty suit. Y'gotta give it to a brotha, he sure knows how to dress!"

I pictured him as I saw him last, cowboy strut aiming for the elevator, shoulders back as those beefy arms swayed forward and back, as his long muscular legs propelled him with each easy stride. "Yeah," I sighed. "I guess."

"He's waving at me, the fool, flashing that million dollar smile. Wonder what the hell he wants?"

"Girl, get outta that car. Grab your briefcase and get up here before he tries to smooth talk *you* with his bullshit."

"Hold on," Lia said. "I'll just keep talking to you, make him think I'm into some big important business, too busy for the likes of him."

She went silent for a minute, long enough that I almost said, "Lia? You still there?" I never got the chance, though, because she whispered, "Now, what's he talking to the UPS man about?" Lia laughed. "What the hell!"

"Girl, what's so funny?"

"You wouldn't believe what I'm looking at. Only in Balti-more! You near a window?"

"Yeah..."

"Look toward the parking lot," Lia said.

I stepped up to the windows and peered out.

"See this chick? Blonde wig, fake fur, clear stilettos, sun-glasses when the sun is barely out and...and *gloves* on?" Lia laughed again. "What you bet she's wearing some grill, too."

My turn to laugh. "Girl, you're too funny. Yeah I see her and you're right...only in Baltimore."

Lia laughed along with me. "Tell me about it. Well, let me get upstairs."

I headed back into the receptionist's area. "I'll be in the ladies room, freshening up." Almost as an afterthought, I tacked on, "You get me lotsa moolah outta that mutha, I'll buy *you* a pair of those clear-heeled—"

Gunshots interrupted my joke. Two in quick succession, then a third.

"What the hell was that?"

Silence on the other end of the phone.

"Lia? What's going on out there, girl?"

All I could hear was quiet gasping. I froze. The seconds ticked silently by. Surely Lia hadn't been...I couldn't make myself think it.

I ran back to the windows, but couldn't see anything other

than the chick with the crooked blond wig, running like Flo Jo, while looking over her shoulders.

Then the receptionist was beside me, hands over her lips. "What's going on Mrs. Hunter? What was that noise?"

I didn't have time to say anything to calm her down except, "Call 9-1-1. Tell them there's been a shooting in the parking lot." It hit me like a brick to the forehead: Kyle was out there, too!

Running like the devil himself was on my heels, I headed for the elevators. "9-1-1," I shouted, banging on the Down button. "NOW!"

I saw the receptionist grab the phone as the elevator doors closed.

"Come on, come on!" I begged. "Get me down there!" Tears filled my eyes as a sob choked off my words. When I finally reached the lobby after taking the stairs because the elevator was stuck, I caught my breath and raced for the entrance, bumping into businessmen and women crowded around the elevator.

Get the fuck out of my way, you idiots! I screamed in my head. *Didn't you hear the shots? Don't you realize...somebody's been gunned down!.*

Somebody...

Lia? Or...Kyle?

Even before I hit the sidewalk, a small crowd had gathered. I pushed through the busy-bodies. The paramedics were putting Kyle on a gurney. He was bleeding and my heart started beating rapidly. My breath was becoming short and I was breaking into a sweat.

"Move!" I ordered. And when the paramedic held up a hand to block me, I said, "That's my husband...is he...he isn't..."

He laid a hand on my shoulder. "Ma'am, he was shot in the right shoulder. He may have hit his head when he fell, and blacked out. We've got to get him to Hopkins. You can ride in the back of the ambulance if you like."

I stroked Kyle's left hand, dangling from the gurney. I kept stroking his hand, and couldn't help but notice that even unconscious, it seemed powerful. He was still wearing his wedding band and I felt weak in the knees.

"No. I'll follow you." Then I remembered Lia, who'd gone

silent...except for the sickening wet sounds I'd heard before the phone went dead. "Was...was anyone else hurt?"

The paramedic pointed as he climbed into the back of the ambulance. "Lady in the gray Lexus wasn't so lucky. Took a couple of shots to the chest. Poor thing didn't stand a chance." He reached for the door handle. "Friend of yours?"

I nodded. "What...what *happened*?"

"You'll have to ask the police. We're never allowed to touch anything till the crime scene investigators arrive. Since your husband is alive, we can bring him in." He motioned for the driver to head out. "Sorry," he said, then slammed the ambulance door.

The ugly reality of it all snaked around me, choking off my words as the piercing wail of the siren drowned out my cries.

I couldn't wrap my mind around it. Why would anyone want to hurt Lia? Or Kyle, for that matter?

I needed to get it together. Yeah, it had been two long years since I'd been out of the game, but damn it, I was one of the best prosecutors in town. If it hadn't been for the stress, heavy caseloads, and the frustration I felt when criminals received light sentences, I may never have quit to open an antique shop in Georgetown. And yeah, selling trinkets, art and antiques was less pressure, but I missed the adrenaline rush that came with protecting innocent victims and locking up the bad guys. I'd find out who killed Lia, and why, and they'll pay. Big time.

The crowd began to grow, and several TV news trucks were now on the scene, setting up equipment to begin broadcasting for the afternoon news.

I wandered over to Lia's car and fear struck me as I saw shattered windshield fragments all around the car. As I stepped closer I could see Lia's head slumped on the steering wheel. She still had her cell phone clutched in her right hand. I stood frozen to the spot in shock and anguish. I didn't know how much time had passed before a deep voice with a New York accent said, "Stay behind the yellow tape."

I hadn't realized I'd ducked under the crime scene tape. Now, it was all I could do to focus because the only thing I could see was Lia. "Oh, I'm...I'm sorry, sir."

"Detective Harris, I'm with the Baltimore City PD," he said. "And you are?" Frowning, he put the tip of his pen to his notebook.

"I'm, ah...I'm Deidre Hunter." I glanced toward Lia's Lexus. "That's my best friend, Lia Reynolds. We were on the phone when it happened, talking about why she was late for our meeting and—"

"Sorry for your loss but I'm sure you understand, this is a crime scene and I can't have you contaminating it. We'll do everything we can to gather evidence to find her killer. You've got my word on that." He waved to a uniformed officer. "You'll need to come to the station for further questioning if you saw or heard anything before she was killed."

"No need to drive me there. I can get to the station on my own." I stood, arms folded, staring him down. "But I'm not going anywhere before I at least get answers to a few preliminary questions."

He grinned a little, then chuckled. "Such as?"

Go ahead, I thought, make fun of me. He'd take a different attitude when he found out what I used to do for a living. "Such as, did you find any shell casings? Fingerprints? Any indication if this was deliberate, or a random shooting?"

His smile grew. "It's only been a few minutes, Miss Hunter. Give us some time, so we can be thorough." The smile vanished and a hard edge cut into his voice. "Meet me at the station in half an hour so I can find out more about this, ah, *conversation* you and the victim were having when this whole thing went down."

"Half an hour, my ass," I spat. "I used to be a prosecutor. I know how long things like this take. If it's all the same to you, I'll wait right here."

Then I thought about Kyle, all alone and bleeding, and in who knows what condition at the hospital. "All right fine," I said, grabbing his notebook. I scribbled my name, address and phone number on the faint blue lines and handed it back. "My husband was shot, too, and is on his way to the hospital. I'm heading over there right now, so you can call me, let me know when I should come to the station."

Both brows rose high on his forehead as he said, "Will do."

It dawned on me that someone would have to inform Lia's parents. "How the hell am I going to tell her mom and dad that their only daughter was shot, that she's..." I swallowed. "How?"

"Don't worry about that. We'll take care of notifying her family. Now, I know it's hard, even with your background but you gotta let us do our work." He held up the crime scene tape, his not-so-subtle hint that I was dismissed. A second passed, then two, before he realized I had no intention of leaving right then. Dropping the tape, he said, "Have it your way, then. But what if the doctors need you to sign consent forms, so they can do whatever they need to do?" He pulled a pair of latex gloves from his front pocket and snapped them on, one at a time. "You know, I'm right."

Yes, I did, but damn him, I wasn't about to admit it. "Fine, I'll leave. I'll be at Hopkins, doing my wifely duties. Put *this* in your book, detective: If I don't hear from you soon, I'll hound the hell out of you."

"Y'know, Mrs. Hunter," he said. "I believe you." And then he turned his back to me and said to another officer, "Where are the crime lab guys? Guess I gotta pick up their slack."

As I worked my way back to Hardwick's office to get my handbag, something caught my eye. A black matchbook, poking out from under Lia's right front tire. Scanning the scene to make sure no one saw me, I bent down and tucked the matchbook into my jacket pocket. I knew I should give it to Detective Harris, but I'd worked with his type before. A know-it-all if ever I saw one. One of those guys who didn't like any evidence unless he found it himself. If the matchbook had anything to do with Lia's murder, I would find out.

I then stood up, walked around to the front of the car and curiously watched Detective Harris in action. He was calm, pensive, and in control as he gave orders to the other police officers to push back the crowd away from the crime scene. As he bent down to put an evidence marker next to a shell casing, he threw his trench coat back exposing his gun on his right hip. He turned his black baseball cap backwards on his head showing he was a New York Yankees fan. He slowly got up and then tapped his pen against his nicely groomed goatee as if contemplating his next move. I admired the way he worked, and if this were any other occasion, maybe this chiseled face caramel eye candy would be just my type.

CHAPTER 2

IN THE MIDST OF ALL the craziness, I waded through the remaining gawkers and went back to Hardwick's office to get my handbag. As I got off the elevator and walked into the office, I saw the receptionist bent over the left side of her desk frantically looking for something in her drawer. The phone lines were ringing off the hook and she didn't make a move to answer them.

"Don't mean to interrupt, but are you okay?" I asked as I got closer to her.

She turned, startled. "Oh, hi Mrs. Hunter. I'm stressed right now. Just trying to find my pills to calm my nerves."

"Yeah, I know the feeling." I shook my head, still numb from what I'd seen downstairs.

"Not much I can do until I calm down. These phones can wait," she said as she went back to tossing items around in the drawer.

I looked over in the area where I had left my handbag and it wasn't there. "Um, did you move my bag? It was on the chair over there," I said, pointing to the chair next to the magazine rack.

"Ah, yeah." She pulled it out from under her desk. "Here you go. Just wanted to make sure it was safe."

I took my handbag and quickly checked to make sure everything was there. "Thanks, I appreciate that." I turned to walk away, but then looked back at her. "Let Mr. Hardwick know that we'll have to reschedule the settlement conference."

She nodded her head. "I'll tell him. Just give us a call when you're ready."

"Sure will." I said and left the office.

I walked out of the building and headed toward the parking lot with my car keys in hand. As I got closer, I unlocked the car doors remotely. I got inside and sat silently for a moment. Reaching into my jacket pocket, I pulled out the matchbook to take a closer look. The name "Kitty Kat Club" was emblazoned on the cover in raised red lettering with a silhouette of a woman with a pole between her legs. I stared at the name of the club because it seemed familiar to me. I suddenly remembered that I had read something about a shootout between some patrons about three months ago outside of the club.

My mind then shifted to the mysterious woman in the blond wig who fled the scene. I wondered whether she was connected with the club. I needed to get more details about who she was, what she knew and whether she had anything to do with the murder of my best friend and the shooting of my soon to be ex-husband. Only a guilty person or someone who saw what happened and feared being a witness would flee a crime scene. Which was she?

I flipped the matchbook over and stared at the phone number on the back. I took a deep breath before punching in the numbers on my cell phone.

After four rings, a husky voice answered, "Kitty Kat Club."

"Ah, yes. Um...you looking to hire any new dancers?" I asked, clearing my throat and trying to sound street.

"Yup, today must be your lucky day. One of dem hos just up and quit last night," the man said.

"When can I come in to see the manager 'bout the job?"

"Wednesday, nah, make dat Friday. Yeah, two o'clock. What's your name baby girl?"

I thought quickly. "Private Dancer."

"Hmm, nice stage name. I like dat. When you get 'ere, come 'round back and ask for Marvin. Aight."

"Yeah, aight. What's your name?"

The phone went dead before I got an answer. I held it in my

hand and wondered what the hell I was getting myself into. I am a pretty good dancer, but what did I know about being that type of dancer? Well, no stopping me now. I knew just the right person to call.

I hit speed dial on my cell phone. The phone rang two times before she answered. "Hey girl, what's up with you?" Angela said in a perky voice.

"Nothing much. What you doing?" I tried to sound as normal as I possibly could to hide the hurt I was feeling. I needed to devise a plan and didn't need Angela advising me against it.

"Just getting back from the gym and I'm starving."

"Oh, getting your work out on huh?"

"Yeah, gotta maintain my girlish figure," she said. "Why? You finally thinking about joining the living? Heart be still." She laughed.

I laughed too. "Yeah, something like that. Still taking those exotic dance lessons on Saturdays?"

"Ah, yes. Have to keep my man on his toes."

"Care if I tag along and check it out for myself?"

Angela's line beeped. "That's cool. But, hey, I gotta take this call coming in. Meet me at my house tomorrow at noon and we can ride together. Okay, bye!" she said before rushing off the phone.

I didn't get the chance to tell her that Lia had just been killed and that Kyle was injured and in the hospital. She would be pissed I had taken on the job of solving this case and not involving her somehow. Even though she had her own business, she liked living on the edge and often joked about us being the black Thelma and Louise, two road warriors.

I sighed, turned off the phone and threw it into my handbag. I started the engine and made my way through traffic to check on Kyle at the hospital.

It was almost ten o'clock and the morning temperature was slowly rising when I arrived at Hopkins. The visitor's parking lot was full but I got lucky when I saw an elderly couple about to leave. I waited patiently as I watched the driver lift the woman from the wheel chair and place her in the front passenger seat. He closed the door, then folded the wheel chair, popped the trunk and laid it inside. When he turned to head to the driver's side, he stopped and smiled in my direction. I nodded and gave him enough room to pull out of his space. The sight of that couple warmed my heart as I had envisioned Kyle and me growing old and living a long happy life. But sadly, that was not to be.

I walked up toward the entrance of the hospital and made it to the reception desk where I stood in line behind distraught friends and family members asking questions about their loved ones. The receptionist was pleasant as she looked up the patient's information and directed the visitors to the designated floor or waiting area.

"Hi. I'm Deidre Hunter," I said. "I'm here about my husband, Kyle Hunter. Can you tell me what room he's in?"

She checked her computer and then looked up at me. "He's still in surgery and it could be a couple hours before you can see him."

"Are there any papers for me to sign?"

"No. Everything's fine. His mother signed off on the necessary papers."

I forgot that Jaynie worked in radiology at the hospital and must have been on shift when the paramedics brought him in. I hoped she didn't blame me for her precious son getting hurt.

"Oh, okay. Is Jaynie still here?"

"Let me check. Her shift ended an hour ago but I'm sure she's around here somewhere." She picked up the phone. "Give me a sec. I'll try to page her." "Thanks."

"Hi, this is Celia from reception. Is Jaynie in the lounge area?" she asked. She cupped the phone and said to me, "They're checking."

After a few seconds she was back on the phone. "Okay, tell her that Deidre is here and wants to see her. Thanks," she said and then hung up.

"You can have a seat over there in the waiting area." She pointed to the left of the hallway. "Jaynie will be down in a minute. Please sign in."

After signing in, I tapped my fingers on the counter. "Thanks," I said before walking over to the waiting area.

An hour went by and I had already snacked on a cereal bar, drank my second cup of coffee, chatted with some of the other visitors and thumbed through several magazines. I sat with my left leg shaking up and down. A nervous habit I had developed when I got anxious especially now that I was waiting for Jaynie to give me a status report.

The television distracted me for a while as I watched highlights of the presidential debates and the candidates making their last minute efforts to rally more voters. I was smiling at the thought of the country having its first African-American President until I felt a gentle tap on my left shoulder. I looked up and saw Jaynie. She had been crying, I could tell from the puffiness under her eyes.

"Hey, Jaynie," I said, getting up to give her a hug.

"Hi Deidre," she said, releasing herself from my embrace. "What happened out there today?"

"My lawyer was murdered...shot to death and Kyle may have gotten in the way," I said as I held her right hand and motioned for her to sit next to me.

Jaynie shook her head in dismay. "Sorry to hear about your friend."

"Thanks." I took a deep breath as I choked back the tears. "So how's Kyle? What did the doctors say?"

"They said he's lucky, no major arteries were damaged. I'm just glad my son's alive."

"That's great news. How much longer is he going to be in surgery?"

"A few more hours."

"Well," I said, getting up from the chair. "Maybe we can grab some lunch to kill some time."

"Sounds good. You buying?" Jaynie asked.

"Yes. What's good around here?"

"It's too cold to go back outside. The cafeteria is good."

"Doesn't matter as long as I can get a good burger and some fries," I said as my stomach growled with hunger. It was now late afternoon and I had to force myself to eat something after the events from earlier this morning.

"Sounds like you're starving," Jaynie said, and laughed.

"Yup. Lead the way."

"After we eat I have to go pick up the grandkids."

"That's okay. I'll stay here until Kyle gets out of surgery."

Lunch was very pleasant. Jaynie talked about her latest knitting class and gossiped about the neighbors and their new additions to their homes. We headed back to the waiting area where she left to get the grandkids and I went to inquire about Kyle once again. This time I was told that he was out of surgery and was heavily sedated, but I could see him briefly.

My cell phone starting buzzing in my bag. I looked down to see an unfamiliar number on the caller ID.

"Hello?"

"Ah...Mrs. Hunter, this is Detective Harris. We're still waiting at the station for your statement."

"Well, I'm at the hospital and I'm afraid it'll be some time before I can get there."

"An hour, two hours, how long?" he said in an irritated voice.

"Don't get snippy with me detective," I snapped back. "I'll get there as soon as I can, if not, then I'll have to see you tomorrow."

"Just try to get here today if you can. It's always best to get statements while everything is still fresh in your mind."

"I'll do my best."

"Okay," he said, and then ended the call.

I quickly put my cell phone away after reading the signs around the hospital prohibiting the use of cellular phones beyond a certain point. I took the elevator to Kyle's room and knocked gently on the door before walking in. Kyle was resting peacefully. I pulled up a chair and sat with him for about fifteen minutes before I heard him groaning. I reached for another blanket to cover him up and then gently stroked his hair. I always loved the texture of his hair and I noticed that he was beginning to thin in the middle of his head. I knew he would be taking care of that very soon because he was so vain.

"Deidre..." He groaned as his eyes kept fluttering to come open.

"Yeah, Kyle, I'm here. Try not to talk too much."

"It hurts," he said.

"Shhh. I know. You gotta save your strength."

"Hmm, okay. I need my stuff. I have to call the office. I have to..."

"Stop worrying so much. I'll swing by your place and get some things."

His eyes were now completely opened and focused on my face. He then looked around the room and frowned once he realized that he was in a shared room.

Here it comes. I braced myself for his tirade.

"What the fuck? Why am I sharing this room?"

I laughed. "You never change, do you? It's the only one they had available. But I'll make arrangements to move you to a private one very soon," I reassured him.

He smiled and said, "You always take good care of me."

"Yeah." I patted his hand. "Well, let me get out of here, I need to get to the police station to give my statement."

"Why? Do you know anything about the shooting?" he asked.

"Kyle..." I said, "Lia's dead." I felt a lump in my throat when I said those words. It made it all too real.

"What?" His eyes bulged out at me.

"Yes, she's gone." I held back a tear.

"Oh, Deidre. I'm so sorry."

"I'll be okay. Let's take care of you now," I said, trying to be strong.

Kyle asked me to stay another fifteen minutes. I obliged, but then he demanded to make the calls to his office and to some of his clients. No one would have thought he had just been shot and barely out of surgery. He was such a workaholic when it came to his hedge fund company. While I admired his drive, sometimes he just went too far.

CHAPTER 3

SATURDAYS HAD ALWAYS BEEN MY favorite day to sleep in. I didn't have a lot of errands to run and I really needed my rest today, especially after giving my statement late yesterday afternoon at the police station, coming home, and then drowning myself in a half bottle of Merlot. It dulled the pain, but left me mentally, physically and emotionally drained. Even though I took two aspirins before falling asleep, my hangover still needed attention. No such luck, as I was suddenly awakened by a leaf blower revving and raring to go at seven in the morning.

"Ahhh." I pulled myself up from the sofa and swung my legs onto the floor. They felt heavy and my whole body ached from not sleeping comfortably in my bed. I hung my head between my legs, closed my eyes and massaged my temples with my fingertips. It was a dulling pain and I cursed the workers for starting so early in the morning, but I guess it forced me to get a head start with my day.

I got dressed quickly, got some orange juice, picked up a croissant from the bread basket and walked over to my home office that was shielded by curtained French doors. This was my safe haven and as I sat down in my swivel chair, I picked up my pen and kept tapping it against my desk—another nervous habit of mine when I'm in deep thought.

Tap. Tap. Was Lia's murder a case of mistaken identity?

Tap. Tap. Was this a gang initiation?

Tap. Tap. Was she murdered because she was a witness to a crime?

I was spinning around in the chair, when my cell phone rang. I spun around and steadied myself before answering.

"Hello."

"Good morning. Mrs. Hunter?"

"Yes," I said politely after recognizing the voice.

"It's Detective Harris. I apologize for calling so early but do you have a minute?"

"Yes. Have there been any new developments?"

"Right to the point as usual," he said.

"Well?"

He chuckled. "Okay. I think we may have a break in the case."

I perked up. "Go on."

"Got a tip last night. The caller operates a homeless shelter near the harbor and um, one of the regulars came in wearing a blond wig and a fur coat."

Pulling out a notepad, I started taking notes. "Wow. Did they say anything else?"

"Yes and they're coming in tomorrow morning to look at some mug shots. I know it's against protocol and against my better judgment, but do you want in?"

"Do you have to ask?" I smirked. "What time should I be there?"

"Eleven."

When I hung up the phone, I finally felt we were on our way to getting some answers.

I arrived at the police station with a few minutes to spare. I sat in my car, flipped down the mirror to check my hair, fixed my hat and ran my fingers over my teeth to get rid of excess lipstick that I had put on in a hurry. I got out of the car, paid for parking and then ran up the steps to the station. As I pulled the doors open to walk up to the desk officer, I saw a police officer hauling a suspect away from the booking area. The scar on the suspect's neck stopped me dead in my tracks. I popped up my collar, pulled my hat close over my eyes and stepped back behind a column. When I thought they were out of sight, I peeked around the column and made sure that the coast was clear before I took another step. My heart raced and I felt a tightness in my chest because this same suspect had vowed to "carve a puzzle" out of my face for sending him to jail on a drug charge a few years ago. So I couldn't stand to face him in this or any other setting.

"G'morning. I'm here to see Detective Harris. He's expecting me." "Your name ma'am?" the desk officer asked.

"Deidre Hunter."

"He's in the interrogation room, down the hall, second door on your right."

"Thanks," I said, walking briskly down the hall.

I found the door and knocked twice. Detective Harris opened the door with a broad smile and stepped aside to let me in.

"Good to see you, Mrs. Hunter."

"You can drop the formality, just call me Deidre."

"Okay, Deidre. Please have a seat. I'll have you watch through the glass while I ask the witness a few questions and determine whether she got a good look at the woman wearing the blond wig. We'll see what shakes."

I nodded, took a seat and waited. I watched Detective Harris diligently asks the witness several questions before summoning the sketch artist to make a facial composite of the suspect. The witness told Detective Harris that the woman in the blond wig and coat had ditched the items in a dumpster and thought that she was either drunk or asleep and didn't get a good look at her.

My attention was focused on the interrogation until Angela kept blowing up my cell phone. I finally answered.

"Hey girl. What's up?" I whispered.

"Well, are you on your way to my house or what?" Angela said with an attitude.

"Oh, shit. Yeah, I had completely forgotten. But hey, I always keep some gym gear and an extra pair of heels in my trunk. Be there soon."

"Remember class starts at one o'clock, so hurry up. 'Cause you know I'll leave you."

I laughed. "I know."

Detective Harris left the room with the sketch artist still working on a composite. He came into the room just as I was putting away my cell phone. I placed my bag on the floor and looked up at him.

"Do we have something to go on?" I asked.

"Yes."

"Do you think this woman has a record?"

"I'll definitely check our database." He placed his hand on his chin and cocked his head to the side.

"Penny for your thoughts?"

He smiled. "Hmm. Something like that."

"I don't like games, so spit it out."

"If I find out she has a record can I tell you over coffee?" he asked.

"There you go breaking the rules again but a simple call will do," I said, sensing he was trying to hit on me. I got up from the chair and snatched my bag from the floor.

"I see you are running off again," he remarked with a raised eyebrow.

"Yes and what of it?"

"I thought you wanted to be up to speed with everything?"

"I do, but..." I paused and headed toward the door.

"Hey, how's your husband?"

I stopped and turned to face him. "Recovering."

He came closer and whispered in my ear, "I'll reach out to you when I know more."

"Looking forward to it," I said, and walked out of the room.

I raced over to Angela's house only to find her already seated in her white Honda Accord, ready to go. Being on time was very important to her. She would always tell me that being punctual was a sign that you cared about someone else's time.

Angela and I met three years ago when I volunteered for a food drive in Baltimore City, and since then we would make time to grab lunch, dinner, movies or plays when our schedules allowed it. Standing at five feet two inches tall, with a caramel latte complexion, she had a sharp tongue and said whatever was on her mind. She was a shrewd businesswoman who ran her own day spa for little girls and her time became even more precious in trying to keep the doors open.

So I hurriedly got my gym gear from my trunk and jumped

into her car, fastened my seatbelt and didn't say a word during the fifteen minute ride to the dance studio. After checking in, I went to the women's locker room and quickly changed into a white tank top, black shorts, and a pair of heels. When we walked into the dance studio, Angela guided me to the front of the class where the poles were already set up for us to get our groove on. The class began filling up with housewives and I saw a few younger women huddled together waiting for the instructor's entry.

"Hey, ready to shake your booty?" Angela asked, as she was bopping her head to the music on her iPod.

"Yeah. Who's teaching the class?"

Angela unplugged one of her earphones. "Cheena, she's got some Latin flava, she'll be here soon." She went back to snapping her fingers and shaking her head to her music.

At almost one o'clock in the afternoon, Cheena came flying in like a gust of wind with her blond curly bob moving from side to side. She was wearing black low rider spandex shorts, clear stiletto heels with ankle straps, and a pink halter top revealing her surgically enhanced chest. She threw her crochet bag on the floor and quickly plugged her iPod into the sound system and out blasted "Doin' It" by LL Cool J.

I started grooving to the music when Cheena turned around facing the class, and flashed a big smile while adjusting the microphone pack around the back of her waist and the headset on top her head and in front of her mouth.

"Welcome to Sexpressions. My name's Cheena. Got any virgins in the class?"

"Huh?" I said with a puzzled look on my face.

Angela nudged me. "She means any new people. Go on girl, put your hand up, don't be shy."

"All right," I said, putting my hand up.

"Welcome!" Cheena said.

A round of applause erupted around the class and I felt the energy from everyone ready to go.

"We're gonna warm it up. Remember we are here to get a great work out, overcome our inhibitions and find our inner sexuality."

Someone from the back of the class shouted, "Yes!"

Prince's "Sexy M.F." came on next and Cheena started swaying her hips right and left then bending over with her palms touching the floor. The class followed her every move and began finding their own inner sensuality.

"Now ladies grab the pole, start stroking it like ahhh...well, you know..." Cheena laughed.

At first, I was a little apprehensive but after forty-five minutes of gyrating, bending, sliding up and down the pool, grinding and booty bumping, I became empowered and my movements became more fluid. Everyone in the room worked up a sweat and learned some new moves too.

"Okay. *Se acabó*," Cheena said, crossing her hands across her face and then flaring them out to the left and then to the right. "Time to cool down."

The class cooled down to Janet Jackson's "I Get Lonely" and was dismissed.

"Whew, girl, that was a workout," I said, wiping my brow and then taking a sip from my water bottle.

"Yup, I told you. Cheena's no joke," Angela said as she play-fully slapped me on the back with her towel.

"Gotta agree with that."

"So what's up with you suddenly showing some interest in this class?"

"Well, I felt I was in a rut for my exercise routine and wanted to shake things up," I said, lying through my teeth. Little did Angela know this was a crash course in learning some moves so I could make a good impression at my audition at the Kitty Kat Club.

"Hmm, right. Sounds like you're thinking about getting your freak on!"

I laughed. "I'm pleading the fifth."

Angela and I grabbed lunch at Wendy's on our way back from the dance studio. During the ride to her house, I told her that I would definitely take the class again. We hugged goodbye and then I got into my car. I had to make another stop at Kyle's place in Fell's Point, a historic waterfront community located near the Inner Harbor, to pick up some of his things when I heard my cell phone beeping. I forgot that I had left it in the car when I jumped into Angela's car to go to the studio.

I had two unchecked voicemails. The first was from my hair-dresser reminding me of my hair appointment on Tuesday, and the second was from Lia's mother. She sounded frantic and was talking rapidly throughout the message. I had to replay it a couple of times to make sense of her garbled words. I managed to hear her say that I needed to meet her at Lia's condo immediately. Something serious must have happened.

I got off the phone and hurriedly made my way over to Federal Hill, a hillside neighborhood easily seen from the Inner Harbor, to see what fire I had to put out. Going to Kyle's would have to take a back seat to a mother who had just lost her only daughter.

When I arrived at Lia's condo, I banged on the door and Mrs. Reynolds poked her head out, looked left and right, before pulling me in and slamming the door.

"What's going on Mrs. Reynolds?" I asked.

Mrs. Reynolds was fidgeting around before she said, "I found this in Lia's dresser." She held up a large business sized envelope.

"What is it?"

She handed me the envelope before plopping down on the sofa. "See for yourself."

I carefully opened the envelope and read its contents. I felt my face turning red with anger as I sat next to Mrs. Reynolds, who began crying uncontrollably. I reached over and gave her a hug. She buried her head on my shoulder and cried even more.

"Mrs. Reynolds, I'm so sorry. Didn't know that Lia was the key witness in a robbery homicide. She didn't tell me." I shook my head and wondered who Taevon Jackson, the accused, was.

Mrs. Reynolds lifted her head from my shoulder and wiped her nose with her sleeve. She sniffled, before asking, "Do you think she got killed because she was going to testify?"

"I don't know," I said getting up. "But I'll check into it."

"Promise me you'll be careful. I don't want to lose you too. You're like a daughter to me." She embraced me.

I smiled, patting her on her back. "Is there anything you want me to help you with while I'm here?"

"If you don't mind contacting some of her friends," she sniffled again, "that would be great."

"No problem."

I stuffed the envelope in my bag and made a mental note to make a copy before handing it over to Detective Harris. I spent the next thirty minutes helping Mrs. Reynolds gather some of Lia's belongings including Lia's address book and escorted her to her car.

"Call me if you need anything."

Mrs. Reynolds nodded her head, waved and then drove off.

When I got to my car, I called Detective Harris who picked up on the second ring.

"Harris," he answered.

"It's Deidre. I got some information that you need to see."

"Okay, want me to meet you somewhere?"

"I have to pass the police station before I jump on 95. So I'll meet you there." I sighed.

"Are you okay?"

"Not really. I'll explain when I get there in about twenty minutes."

"Cool."

Parking was atrocious in downtown Baltimore, especially near the police station. I didn't feel like driving around or even paying ten dollars to park in the garage for just a brief visit, so I double parked in front of the building. Within five minutes, Detective Harris came running down the steps and around to the driver's side window. There were a lot of impatient drivers honking their horns for me to move, but Detective Harris just flashed them his badge and told them to go around my car. I leaned out the car window.

"Oh, so you direct traffic too, huh?"

He smiled and I could see his dimples. "When I have to. So, what you got for me?"

I was hesitant to turn over the envelope to him, but I knew it was the right thing to do. No sense tampering with evidence even more and risk losing my law license.

"Here." I handed him the envelope. He tucked it under his arms. "Oh, um...I have something else for you." I hesitated for a moment before reaching into the car's console and pulling out the matchbook.

"What's this?" he asked.

"I, ah...found this near Lia's car. I picked it up, put it my jacket pocket. Forgot it was there. Could mean something," I said, innocently hunching my shoulders.

He gave me a quizzical look as if doubting the truthfulness of my statement. "And you're just now handing it over?"

"Yeah, like, how 'bout you're welcome? Geez."

"Humph." He stepped away from the car and lightly pounded on the top of it telling me to get going.

"Keep in touch," I said, before pulling into traffic. At the traffic light, I glanced at the rear-view mirror and watched him staring at the matchbook.

CHAPTER 4

LIA'S DEATH HAD MY MIND going in a million directions. To shut out the inner and outer chatter, I decided to meditate and clear my head. I picked up my yoga mat which was propped up against a wall in the living room, laid it on the floor, and sat cross-legged with my hands in prayer position in front of my heart center. My eyes were closed and I inhaled and exhaled several breaths to usher in a sense of calmness. That didn't last long because I began to feel restless. I uncrossed my legs, got up, walked upstairs to my bedroom, and began organizing my closet.

After I finished neatly folding my sweaters and putting them away, I began organizing my shoe closet. Somehow, this seemed to take my mind off things until I stumbled upon a shoe box covered with a colorful wrapping paper. I opened it and found pictures of Lia and me when we were in law school together at Georgetown University. I sat on the floor with the box between my legs and smiled as I pulled out one picture at a time.

We had beauty, brains, and charm, a killer combination which made us the envy of some of the other female law students who didn't know us. For the guys, it was a challenge to get us into bed. We studied for finals together, argued mock trials, hung out at parties celebrating the end of the semester and crammed for the bar exam. She was my maid of honor, counseled me when Kyle gave me grief and offered a shoulder to cry on when my mother passed away from cancer. She was truly my best friend and I miss her dearly.

My eyes began to mist and a tear fell on the last picture I held in my hand of us making goofy faces at the camera. I wiped the tear away with my thumb. Although I was sad and hurting, I had a job to do. I snapped out of memory lane, jumped to my feet, grabbed the remote and turned on the CD player. Time was of the essence and I needed to practice my dance moves so that I could get the job at the Kitty Kat Club. I began dancing to the sensual sounds of Rick James and Teena Marie when I heard the doorbell. Ding, Dong. Ding, Dong. Whoever it was kept ringing the bell and this irritated me.

I came downstairs, tiptoed to the door, peered through the peep-hole and saw my neighbor, Ms. Benita. Although it was cold outside, she wearing a burgundy terrycloth house robe, pink rollers in her hair, tennis shoes and her glasses barely hanging on her nose. She was a retired school teacher and spent most of her days peeking through windows, sometimes using binoculars, and gossiping. She knew all the neighbors and kept a notebook of their transgressions: who was cheating on whom with the cable man, who lost their job and began drinking, who got arrested by the police and the list went on. She was her own self-appointed president of the neighborhood watch program. I didn't mind her stories and found them entertaining at times, but I was not in the mood for her today and wondered what brought her to my door at nine o'clock in the morning.

I took a deep breath before opening the door and stepping outside to greet her with a forced smile.

"Yes, Ms. Benita. What can I do for you so early in the morning?"

"Well, chile...," she said with her left hand on her hip and a newspaper in her right hand, "that paper boy threw your paper on my lawn again." She fidgeted a little. "Hmm, heard about your friend Ms. Lia. You holding up all right?"

Here she goes needling for information. "Hanging in there," I said, extending my hand to her. "My paper."

"Oh, here you go," she said.

I took the paper and was about to head inside before she stepped closer to me.

"So, um...you gonna invite me in for some coffee so you can tell me what happened?"

"Not today, Ms. Benita. Coffee maker's on the blink and I

have a headache," I lied.

"I understand. Well, okay then, take care." She reached in for a hug and patted me on the back. "Sorry for your loss, chile."

I embraced her. "Thanks, you enjoy the rest of your day, Ms. Benita."

She chuckled. "You know I will, got so much to do." She shuddered and pulled her robe a little tighter.

"Hurry on back inside. Don't want you catching a cold," I said.

"Yeah, you're right Ms. Dee. Call if you need anything." She folded her arms and walked back to her house.

That was a really nice gesture from Ms. Benita, but somehow I felt she was prying for some inside information which she would tweak into a juicier tale to share with her other retired cronies over coffee and muffins.

⁓

When I arrived at Frederick's of Hollywood in Glen Burnie, it was filled with early afternoon shoppers getting a head start for the holiday, including men picking out naughty outfits and nervously looking over their shoulders. I chuckled to myself and wondered whether those outfits were gifts for their wives or mistresses for being naughty or nice. I kept browsing around the store before I pulled a couple of Parisian lace corsets and a black sheer lace trim baby doll outfit from the racks and walked into the dressing room. Each time I tried on an outfit, I felt transformed into a sex diva ready for my audition at the Kitty Kat Club.

I was admiring myself in the full length mirror when someone knocked on the dressing room door.

"Yes," I said politely.

"Hi. Do you need any extra sizes, different colors?" the sales associate asked.

"Um, sure. Let me try that sexy kitten costume in red, the one advertised in the window. Size eight."

A few moments went by before the sales associate handed me the outfit over the door. "Here you go. This is nice...special occasion?" she asked. I sighed.

"Okaaay, well, how do they fit?"

"Tell you in a minute," I said, wiggling my body to fit into the outfit. "You know, they'd look really nice with some black thigh high boots or ankle cuff sandals," she said through the door.

"Wow. Never thought of that. You seem to know your stuff. Been working here a while?" I asked.

The sales associate laughed and then whispered, "Yes, and I'm also a stripper...well an exotic dancer, yeah that's more professional." She laughed again. "This is just my day job."

"What's your name?" I asked, admiring the way I looked in the outfit. "Beatrice, Trixie for short. I know girl, I have no idea what my momma was thinking."

I chuckled. "Nice to meet you, Trixie. I'm Deidre. Got any wigs out there? Might as well go all the way."

"Yeah, I think you would look good in a pixie cut or bob style or even a straight style with bangs. Let's play around with some styles until we find you the perfect fit for the shape of your face."

Trixie scurried away and came back within a few minutes with the items requested. After trying on the sexy kitten costume, I came out of the dressing room and asked her to assist me with the wigs. I was getting into character and loving it. I made my final selections of outfits and settled on the dark brown bob style wig with light brown streaks that complemented my oval face. I was very pleased with Trixie's attentiveness and conveyed those sentiments to the manager who was standing nearby.

"Thanks, Deidre," Trixie said, waving as I headed out the door. "Come back and see us soon."

I waved back at her. "It may be sooner than you think."

I popped open the trunk of my car and tossed in my shopping bags. I hadn't seen Kyle since Friday so I called Jaynie to see how he was doing and whether he needed anything. I slid into my seat, reached for my cell phone and punched in Jaynie's number. She picked up on the third ring.

"Hey Deidre."

"Hi, Jaynie. How ya doing?"

"All right. Tryin' to make Sunday meal for them grandkids of mine."

"I see you're stuck with all three of them again."

"Yeah, that's how it goes sometimes," she said.

"Where's their momma?" I asked.

"Out with friends."

I hissed. "Must be nice. How's Kyle?"

"Fine. He still wants his clothes," she said, rattling pots and pans in the kitchen before turning on the faucet. "He's not happy about wearing stuff I picked up for him from Wal-Mart. You know how he is."

"Boy, don't I. Well, I'm heading over to his place now and will stop by the hospital to see him after that."

"What about you, how ya doing?" Jaynie turned off the faucet.

"Still can't believe Lia's gone, but...I'm coping for now."

"Well, let me know if you need to talk or anything."

"Okay. Hey, Jaynie...," I said.

"Yeah."

I paused. "Thanks."

"Anytime. Take care, ya hear?"

"I will." I hung up the phone, put my sunglasses on and made my way into traffic to Kyle's place.

During the drive, I wondered why Kyle didn't call to argue with me. I guess he was playing nice since I had just lost my best friend. On any other occasion, he would have cursed me out and thrown a tantrum if I didn't move fast enough on his request. He treated his employees the same way and they feared him. They would jump at his every beck and call and he loved it that way. Other times, he would be as sweet as pie while everyone around him waited for the other shoe to drop. He reminded me so much of Dr. Jekyll and Mr. Hyde.

Parking on a side street, I walked up to his townhouse. I opened the door and found stacks of magazines and comic books on his table wrapped in plastic waiting to be read. I shook my head as this was a very typical habit of his. I then went upstairs to his bedroom and found his travel bag in the closet. I pulled out some boxers, designer sweat pants and T-shirts from his dresser and when I pushed the drawer in to close it, a Polaroid picture fell to the ground. I picked it up and it was picture of Kyle and some woman sitting on his lap with her arms around his neck and her head turned away from the camera. His hand was on her leg and he was grinning like a Cheshire cat.

I held the picture up to the light, but I couldn't make out the image of the woman except that she was dressed in stilettos, a skimpy outfit and had a tattoo of a bunny on her right leg. This picture was probably taken at one of the clubs where he occasionally went to rescue "damsels" in distress. He prided himself on being a champion of their cause and felt it was his duty to show these women a different lifestyle. This created a lot of heated arguments and many fights between us.

I was pissed, but I finished packing his clothes, put the picture in my bag and walked out the door. I marveled at how he would get himself into situations like this over and over again and never thought these women were using him for his money. I had seen pictures of him with lots of women before, but somehow this looked more intimate. Whenever I would find these pictures, he would say if I can't stand looking at them then I shouldn't go snooping around his stuff. He was right and since then I resisted the urge to go snooping. There was no more room for being disrespected regularly as I was finally doing something about it by getting my divorce.

When I got to his room at the hospital, I heard him screaming at the nurse for bringing him the wrong flavor of ice cream. I waited for the nurse to leave and then I peeked in. Kyle smiled and sat up in bed when he saw me.

"Well, it's about time you got back here to see me. What, no hug?" He beckoned to me with open arms.

I walked toward him, leaned in and gave him a hug, but then pulled away when he tried to kiss me on the lips. He laughed, but I didn't think it was funny.

"So how ya feeling?" I asked.

"Glad to be alive," he said as he patted his right shoulder. "Is that my stuff?"

"Yeah, here you go. Want me to put it in the closet?"

"That's fine, you're always taking care of me. You're the best," he said.

I closed the closet door and stood next to the window over-looking the parking lot and admired the leaves changing into vibrant fall colors of orange, red and yellow.

"What's bothering you?" he asked.

"Ah, nothing. Just can't seem to wrap my head around Lia's death. Shooter's still on the loose."

Kyle rolled on his right side and patted the bed. "Come sit."

I obeyed. We chatted while he ate his dinner and read the *Bal-timore Sun*. I moved from the bed and sat in the chair off to the side and absent mindedly flipped through the channels until I settled on watching a rerun of an old sitcom on TV One. When the show ended, I was ready to go.

I stood up and straightened my slacks. "Hey, I need to head home. Lia's funeral is in two days and I have to help her mom with some last minute details."

"Give her my best and let her know how sorry I am that I can't make it."

"I'm sure she'll understand." I picked up my bag and pulled out my car keys.

"Come see me again," he said, holding the newspaper up to his face and dismissing me.

CHAPTER 5

THE DAY OF RECKONING—LIA'S FUNERAL. The mood was somber set against a rather dreary damp kind of day. The wind was gusty, but that didn't stop anyone who loved Lia as a friend, a co-worker and community activist from paying their last respects. I sat with her family in the front pew and her mother held my hand and squeezed it throughout the entire service. Mr. Reynolds tried comforting his wife, but she kept rocking from side to side crying, blowing her nose, all the while not letting go of my hand. She was overcome with grief and so was I, but I tried to be strong for the both of us in between wiping away my own tears. The service was very moving and there were no dry eyes after Lia's uncle sang "Amazing Grace," her favorite song, a cappella.

After the service when the majority of the crowd departed from the gravesite, I remained there rooted in silence. I looked at Lia's grave and saw a single white lily lying on top of the other flowers that were generously tossed in. I mused and knew it had to be Russell, the love of her life. Russell was a musician, freelance writer, and free spirit. He never liked working a nine-to-five gig, as he called it, and spent his time playing at local jazz clubs. He met Lia four years ago at a flower shop near her home when she was shopping for her usual weekly fresh variety bouquet of flowers and a separate bouquet of lilies. Lilies were her favorite and she was amazing at creating beautiful floral arrangements, which added a nice touch to her home. I had no such skills and my home was filled with artificial plants which I had to dust every now and then.

Russell knew how much she loved lilies and always made sure she had a single one on very special occasions to remind her that she was the only one for him. Their bliss lasted for a while, but almost went south when he showed up drunk at her parents' Christmas party a year ago, causing a scene which nearly landed him in jail for disturbing the peace. Lia's parents couldn't understand what she saw in Russell, but all I know was that whenever he wasn't around she was very miserable. Despite that incident, Lia kept on seeing Russell and avoided her parents bumping into him.

I turned around and saw Russell heading up the hill to his car so I ran after him.

"Hey, Russell," I shouted.

He kept moving faster covering a lot more ground with his long legs and I shouted again. He must have heard me this time, because he turned around and started walking toward me.

"Hey, Deidre." He greeted me with a warm hug and a wide smile that caused wrinkles to form around his eyes.

I embraced him and my face brushed against his loose dreadlocks.

"How ya doing?" I asked.

He hung his head down. "I miss my girl."

"I know, we all do."

"Hmm, damn." He thumped his right fist into the palm of his left hand.

"The police are working hard to track down the killer."

"I'm so mad right now, they took my girl. I think I may have to move back to Atlanta, the memories are just too painful here."

"I hear ya. Do what you have to do to get through it."

"Heard your man got injured too."

"He got shot in the shoulder, but he's recovering. He wanted to be here, but the doctors said he needed to rest some more."

He nodded. "He's the lucky one."

"He is. Well, it was good seeing you."

"You too."

"So, back to ATL huh?" I asked.

"Uh-huh, there are a few upcoming artists who want me to write some songs for them. Besides, it gets too cold in Maryland this time of year. I need some warmth in my bones."

"Right."

He tugged at his coat and then laughed. "Well girl, you got my number. Call and check in on a brotha."

"We'll see." I playfully punched him in his arm. "Be well."

"Try to." He threw me the peace sign and trudged up the hill to his car.

Early Friday afternoon, I packed my sexy outfits and got ready for my audition at the Kitty Kat Club. When I pulled up in the back of the club, I saw Detective Harris getting into his ivory pearl Infiniti sedan. Trying not to panic, I slowed down to a halt, ducked down and hoped he didn't see me. Luckily he went in the opposite direction and I quickly parked. I ran to the back door as instructed by the man over the phone and pressed the buzzer. To my surprise, a tall brown-skinned man with a close cut fade opened the door.

"Hey, you Private Dancer?" he asked.

"Yeah, you Marvin?"

He nodded.

I chewed and smacked my spearmint gum with an attitude and tugged at my too tight tank top under my coat with the fur hood. "Just saw a dude leaving outta here. Y'all dancing this early in the afternoon?"

"Nah. Was some cop investigating a shooting that popped off 'bout a week ago."

"What? It's dangerous like dat round 'ere?" I touched my hair and continued smacking my gum.

"Yeah, sumptin' like dat." Marvin stared me up and down with a sparkle in his eyes that made me feel uneasy. He stepped back, held the door open and I slipped in under his arm.

The Kitty Kat Club looked like a dive from the front of the building. But as I walked in, it was quite cozy with small tables for two dressed with black tablecloths and a candle in the center. The walls were painted a deep shade of red and there was a stage in the center of the club with spotlights all around it. The place reeked of cigarettes and spilt beer, but underneath it all I could smell the sweet scent of jasmine incense.

Marvin led me to his office which had a pin-up girl from the sixties on the front of it. His office was neatly organized and he had pictures with some local stars from the *Wire* plastered on the walls. He offered me a folding chair and I sat down. I was nervous and kept shifting my weight. I began to sweat a little and was anxious to see what Marvin was going to do next. He walked behind his desk and sat down in front of his computer. He paused for a moment then commanded that I take off my clothes.

"Girl, let me see what you got," he said in a serious tone.

I looked at him like he was crazy and asked whether this was my audition.

"Yeah, baby girl, let me see you shake it like a salt shaker." Marvin winked, grabbing my hand and guiding me to the stage.

"Um, mind if I change into something else?" I asked nervously.

"Aight, you can change back there. Make it quick girl." He pointed to the ladies room toward the back of the club.

When I made my way back to the stage, I was wearing a black lace corset under my coat, fish net stockings and four inch heels. For an instant, I stood on the stage a bit frozen until the lights came on.

"What's ya flava?" I heard him say over the microphone. I looked up and he was standing in the music booth flipping through the music selections. The spotlights came on and I shielded my eyes from the glare.

"Huh?"

"Whatchu wanna hear?" Marvin's question echoed over the microphone. "Oh, anything by Chaka Khan."

"Cool, we got summa dat," he said.

My hands were sweaty, but when "Ain't Nobody" came blaring out of the music booth, I dried them off on my clothes and then sprang into action. I peeled off my coat, looked at Marvin and silently prayed that the moves I had practiced would be executed flawlessly. I was feeling the sensual rhythm of the music so I closed my eyes and tilted my head back. I sucked on my bottom lip and cupped my breasts with both hands and started gyrating my hips. I was fully immersed in the music and my mind left the room before it was brought back by the sound of Marvin's voice.

"Dayum girl, you got some moves on ya," he said, sucking on a round yellow lollipop.

I opened my eyes, followed the sound of his voice and there he was, sitting on a chair behind me with his eyes soaking up every inch of my body. I turned my back to him, dipped a little lower, bent over with my palms on the floor, looked between my legs and shook my ass in his face.

"Is this whatchu looking for?" I looked him dead in the eyes.

"Yeeaah," he said, licking his lips. "I'ma lovin' dis, show me some more girl."

"Well all right, then." I twirled around and then did a split.

"What girl, hmm, if you can drop it like dat, it's a wrap!" He laughed. "I need you to do your thang this Sunday night."

"You mean I got the job?" I covered my mouth in surprise.

"Yeah, shawty you got the gig. Show up 'round nine, I'ma let you dance two sets."

"Yup, I can do dat. What about the employment application?"

"We can worry about da paperwork when you get 'ere. Hey check it, I gotta roll so show yourself out," he said.

"Yup, thanks see ya then."

"Ain't nothing," he said as he made his way back to his office.

After I changed, there wasn't any time to snoop around because some drunks stumbled into the club and were heading toward me. So I quickly worked my way out the door and into my car. I knew for sure that I was getting in over my head if I started dancing at this night club. I passed the audition with flying colors, Marvin liked what he saw and I was to report on Sunday to shake my booty. I don't know how long I can keep my cover without some help from the streets. Before long, I would find my answer over in the east side of Baltimore in search of Marcusetta.

Marcusetta's neighborhood was the type you prayed that all the traffic lights were green so you could drive through them. It was on the rough side of town, but I showed no fear. I drove through the side alley and saw her sitting on her stoop smoking a cigarette and petting her pit bull, Blackie. Marcusetta was a transplant from Raleigh, North Carolina. She was only sixteen years old when she came to Baltimore to live with her aunt after her mother was killed by a drunk driver. This was ironic because her mother had just celebrated being sober for a year. Marcusetta's father was in jail and the rest of her family were plagued with problems and had no room for her, so her aunt offered to take her in. That was eight years ago.

At first Marcusetta was thriving in high school, but then got mixed up with some neighborhood girls who were runners for drug dealers. Because of her truant behavior, she almost dropped out of high school. It wasn't until one of her friends got killed in a drive by shooting that she became convinced to straighten out her life. After school, she would go to the local recreation center where I used to volunteer two evenings a week. But she couldn't leave the streets. She kept getting into trouble and almost got locked up for assaulting another girl who lived on the block for mouthing off. The police showed up and luckily I was able to talk them out of arresting her.

I rolled my window down, peered over my sunglasses and whistled at Marcusetta. "Hey, chica, what's up?"

Marcusetta who was dressed in khaki pants and a navy blue hooded sweatshirt looked in my direction, but she didn't appear too happy to see me. The lines on her round face were scrunched up in a frown and her expression read *What the hell are you doing here?* Instead she waved, got up and made her way to my car with Blackie barking at her side.

"Hey, whatchu want?" she said in a southern accent.

"Well, now is that the way to greet an old friend of yours?" I laughed.

"Humph, I haven't seen or heard from you in a minute and now you show up at my doorstep. What's the deal now?" Marcusetta scowled.

"Can I at least come in for a few minutes?" I asked politely.

"I thought I'd never see ya again since ya quit your job locking folks up," Marcusetta said, opening the gate and tying Blackie to a post. "Well, aight, come in then." She then waited until I parked the car around the back of her row house and then we walked into a spotless kitchen. Her aunt didn't play when it came to cleanliness and she constantly reminded guests that it was next to godliness.

Marcusetta sat down at the kitchen table and I pulled out a chair and sat next to her. "Okay, what's up? I'm sure you didn't drop by for a cup of sugar."

"No. Um, did you hear about the shooting last week downtown at the Inner Harbor and the suspect is now in the wind?"

"Yeah, what about it?"

"Well, the person they killed was my best friend and the police have no strong leads. So, this is where you come in."

"Damn, I'm sorry Deidre. I'm listening."

"No one knows the streets better than you. You know all the players, hookers, strippers, users—"

"Uh-huh."

"I need you to start casually asking around, kinda like be my ears on the streets."

"I can do that. Got anything to go on?"

"I may have a lead. I found a matchbook near the scene and I did see a woman running down the street wearing a blond wig and a fur coat." I paused. "I don't know why, but I feel she may be connected somehow."

"What's the name of da club?"

"Kitty Kat Club. The thing is I'm going undercover as a dancer to see what I can find out."

"What?" Marcusetta busted out laughing. "Now that's the craziest shit I ever heard. I can't believe that you're entering the underbelly and mixing with real folks."

"Ha. Ha," I responded sarcastically. "This isn't funny. Trust me I got skills," I said, getting up, snapping my right fingers in the air and twirling around.

"So whatchu need me to do?" Marcusetta asked as she leaned in closer.

"I need you to watch my back when I'm leaving the club late at night and have one of your boys in the club as an extra pair of eyes on me."

"Okay, I can do that. Hmm, I know who I can get to go up in that booty joint. My boy Cassius sure loves some ass. He'd be perfect."

"Thanks girl, I knew I could count on you."

"That's it. No payment for my services?"

"You better not even go there, remember you owe me one for cutting a deal for your homeboy Malik."

"Yeah, yeah, you're right. He could be doing some hard time right about now. My bad." Marcusetta got up from the chair and reached out to shake on our deal.

"So we're cool?"

"Yup. I'll *cawl* you when I know something."

"We've been sitting in here for a while and you haven't even offered me anything to drink."

"My bad, forgot my manners."

"I know you got some sweet tea in that fridge," I said.

"Okay, okay, coming right up," Marcusetta said, running to get some glasses from cupboard.

I kicked off my shoes, enjoyed my sweet tea and spent some time chatting about Marcusetta's latest venture, selling cooked food out of her kitchen.

CHAPTER 6

AFTER MUCH PRODDING FROM DETECTIVE Harris, I decided to meet him for coffee around ten, at a Starbucks in Silver Spring to discuss the case. When I walked in, he was sitting at a table reading the *City Paper*. He was casually dressed in faded jeans, a white button-down long-sleeved shirt, black loafers and a black sports jacket. I stopped in front of him and cleared my throat. He looked up and gave me a cute dimpled smile.

"Glad you could make it." He folded the newspaper, laid it on the table, got up and pulled out the chair across from him.

"Yeah," I said while taking off my coat and laying it on the back of the chair. I sat down and rubbed my hands together. "It's cold out."

"Now, what can I get you to warm you up? My treat." Detective Harris stood next to me poised like a waiter with an imaginary pen and notepad ready to take my order.

"Well, uh, since you're paying, I would like a caramel macchiato, a bacon, egg and cheese breakfast sandwich, a—"

"You must be hungry. What size macchiato, tall, grande or venti?"

I laughed. "I see you speak Starbucks. I was just kidding, but I'll take a tall coffee of the day and a slice of marble cake."

"And I see you've got jokes. Be right back," he said.

I clasped my hands and rested my elbows on the table and

watched Detective Harris walk to the register. This man exuded confidence that made him even more sexy and attractive to me. My gaze traveled from his wide shoulders to his butt and then to his strong legs. With a body like that, I'm sure he works out regularly at the gym. If that's the case, this would be a welcomed change, as Kyle hated the idea of going to the gym and working up a sweat since most of his exercise took place in the bedrooms of other women.

Once, when Kyle wasn't in his office, I checked his computer and found an e-mail from a woman who praised him for his bedroom skills, but scolded him for rushing out of her apartment at four in the morning and leaving her door open. I scrolled down and found a few more e-mails from other women thanking him for flowers, dinners, bracelets, and other favors.

When I angrily confronted him; he scolded me and said *"If you can't stand the heat in the kitchen then you should get out."*

And two weeks later, I did just that.

A crash to the floor and someone shouting, "Oh shit, I almost burned myself," snapped me out of my "Kyle-flashback" episode. I looked up and saw a man frantically mopping up his spilt latte from his shirt, the table and then the floor. His breakfast companion tried to help but the man just glared at her. A few patrons snickered and then went back to their conversations. Meanwhile, some of the female patrons were eyeing Detective Harris, even the cashier was staring him down. I just hoped she got our order right.

Detective Harris came back to the table and placed my coffee and marble cake in front of me before he sat down and licked the foam off his latte. He didn't waste any time getting down to business as he opened up his briefcase and took out a file. I wasn't sure what to expect, but I braced myself as I took a bite of my marble cake.

"Well, for starters, we matched the composite sketch and came up with a name."

"And..."

"LaTasha Morgan. Does that name sound familiar to you?" he asked as he showed me a picture of LaTasha.

"Hmm." I searched my mental database while staring at the picture. "No, should it?" I slid the picture back to him.

"She has a record and I thought maybe her file may have come across your desk a time or two when you were at the State's Attorney's office. Anyway, that's all I have right now. I'll try to track her down and—"

"What about the information I gave you about Lia being a witness in that murder case? Could there be a connection?" I stuffed another piece of cake into my mouth and waited for his response.

"Yeah, I'm looking into that, the State's Attorney's office didn't get back to me yet. I guess they are backlogged or something."

"So if that's all you have, why did you insist on us meeting for coffee?"

"What, and miss a chance to see how sexy you look in that cashmere sweater?"

I fought the urge to blush. "And flirting the way you're doing right now..."

"Uh-huh." He finished off his coffee. "Yeah?"

"You do know I'm still married, right?"

"Yep, but soon to be divorced. No better time than the present. Would hate for another brother to step in and take what I want."

"I guess you've staked your claim, huh?"

"I can see it in your brown eyes." He reached over and moved a wisp of my hair.

His touch surprised me and I flinched.

"Detective Harris, you've stepped over the line." I pushed my chair back and quickly jumped to my feet. "We're in the midst of an investigation and all you can think about is getting some ass? Amazing," I said, not wanting to appear too vulnerable.

"Deidre, I'm sorry. I thought I saw a green light. I, uh..."

"Well, you thought wrong." I threw the napkin on my plate and picked up my bag. "Our business is done here." I gave him the evil eye and folded my arms.

"I'm uh...sorry, Deidre. Please don't cause a scene. Sit. Sit. Please."

He appeared embarrassed and against my better judgment, I unfolded my arms and sat down to hear him out. After ordering another round of coffees, Detective Harris began to unload his life story on me.

I learned that he recently moved from Brooklyn, New York about a year ago to Baltimore. He had just lost his wife and he never stopped blaming himself for her death. She was murdered one night when he decided to cover a shift for a fellow officer. When he came home, he found her dead on the living room floor, strangled and then stabbed to death by a serial killer known to the police department as the "Moonlight Strangler."

The case was never solved and he got so tired of chasing after a ghost that he completely withdrew and became unpredictable on the job. The department ordered him to go to psychotherapy, but that didn't do him any good. So, he decided to take up his fraternity brothers' offer to spend a couple of weeks in Baltimore until he figured out his next move. He never left.

I listened intently as he went on.

"Deidre, you ignite a spark in me I thought would never happen after Sierra's death," he confessed.

I was touched. "I see."

"I admire your strength for dealing with your friend's death and your take charge attitude...well, it just turns me on."

He's smooth, I thought. "Well, thanks for the compliments, but I'm not in the market for any romantic liaisons at the moment." I paused. "I need to get myself together to deal with post-divorce issues."

He nodded his head as if he had a clear understanding of where I stood with him.

I pulled up in my driveway after eight in the evening totally exhausted, which seems to be the norm lately. I had spent the majority of the afternoon sitting in a salon chair at Hair This, a Dominican hair salon in Lanham after Marcusetta called and told me that LaTasha used to be a hair dresser at this salon. I was amazed at how quickly Marcusetta was able to get information on the streets right after I gave her LaTasha's name.

When I got to the salon I pretended I needed a wash and set, even though I had just done my hair a couple of days ago. It didn't matter to the stylist, who chatted like the Energizer bunny, that I had a fresh hairdo as long as I forked over fifty dollars at the end of my appointment. It didn't take long for her to give up information about LaTasha without blinking a questioning eye. Turns out LaTasha quit her job when her brother was arrested for murder six months ago. The stylist didn't know the details, but said that LaTasha left in a hurry and moved to Baltimore.

The chatter continued as she placed the nape of my neck on the edge of the shampoo bowl and told me that she heard from another customer that LaTasha was now stripping at a club near the Inner Harbor. Before I could ask the stylist the name of the club, another customer was standing in front of me ready to jump into her chair. When I left the salon, I wondered whether the club could be the *Kitty Kat Club?*

As I walked up the brick walkway to my house, I noticed that the porch light which automatically came on at six in the evening was out. I shook my head and just added it to the list of things that needed to be fixed around the house I procrastinated getting to. I fished my house keys out of my bag and they fell to the ground. I bent down to pick them up fussing under my breath when suddenly I was hit from behind. I fell to the ground and out of instincts I turned around in time to block the next blow that was aiming toward my head. I still had my keys in my hand and jabbed the attacker on the left leg, but that didn't stop the violent kick to my stomach. I doubled over in pain and turned to face the intruder whose face was hidden behind a ski mask. I feared I was going to get kicked again so I curled up in a ball in anticipation for the attack.

Suddenly, I heard a clanking sound across the street and realized it was Ms. Benita putting her trash out. This startled the intruder and he took off into the bushes. I ached, but managed to scream out to Ms. Benita who came running over with her flashlight shining in my direction.

Ms. Benita shouted, "What's going on over there?"

"Heeelp me!"

Ms. Benita dropped her flashlight to the ground and rushed to my side. "Oh lawd, Deidre, what happened? Here let me help you up." She bent down, slipped her arm around my waist and pulled me up.

Breathing heavily, I said, "Someone just attacked me. Did you see him?"

"No, Oh Lawd," Ms. Benita said in a shaky voice as she helped me to my feet. She took me inside the house and sat me on the sofa. She pulled her cell phone from her pocket and dialed 9-1-1 as she checked all the doors. She then went to the kitchen to get a bag of ice for my head, some alcohol wipes for the bruises on my knees, a bottle of water, and some aspirins for the pain.

"Thanks, Ms. Benita. You don't know how grateful I am that you came out at the right time." I held her hand. "I would probably be lying in the morgue and not on my sofa at this very moment."

"It's okay chile. You're safe now," she said, patting my hand.

It's occasions like these which make me appreciate Ms. Benita being the neighborhood's watch dog. I sat up and took the aspirin and told her I would go to the bathroom in a minute to wipe the blood off my knees. She told me I needed to do it soon if I wanted the sofa to retain its tan color. Before I could get up, my cell phone chimed inside my handbag on the floor signaling that I had a text message. Ms. Benita picked it up and gave it to me as I could hardly move.

When I saw the message, my eyes widened and I tensed up. I was warned.

"NEXT TIME YOU WON'T BE SO LUCKY BITCH!"

I quickly turned off my phone.

"What's the matter, Deidre? Is it bad news?"

I tried masking the expression on my face as best as I could. "Oh, it's nothing to be worried about." Ms. Benita gave me a look of concern mixed with a little dread. I tried not to panic, but I was terrified.

When she went to the kitchen to make us some tea until the police arrived, I called Detective Harris. He didn't say much except that he was on his way. Within fifteen minutes, police cars and an ambulance with flashing lights rested in my driveway. No doubt my neighbors were peering through their windows and some were probably huddled together at the edge of their walkways to see what was unfolding. The police knocked on my door and Ms. Benita showed them into the living room where I was lying on the sofa in visible pain. The paramedics inspected me and I assured them that I would be fine and didn't need to be hospitalized.

The police questioned me for a while, asking me if I recalled anything else that could give them a lead on the attacker. I answered their questions to the best of my abilities and told them I had no knowledge why someone would want to hurt me and that I couldn't identify the attacker, except that I was able to leave a gash on their left leg with my keys. They insisted that I spend the next couple of nights elsewhere with family or friends. I told them I would be fine and safe with my alarm system.

At the end of the police questioning, Ms. Benita told the officer that she had something to add to the statement.

"Officer, um...at around six this evening I saw a suspicious vehicle parked around the corner when I took my dog out to do his business."

"Was anyone inside the vehicle?" the officer asked.

"Yes, there was a man sitting in the driver's seat wearing a gray hooded sweatshirt and sunglasses although the sun had already gone down. He was reclined in the seat and had his hands behind his head."

"What did you do when you saw him?"

"I took the long way back to my house but wrote down the license plate number." She opened her little notebook and gave him the information.

"Ma'am, that's great information. You're very attentive to your surroundings. Wish more folks could be like you," the officer said.

Ms. Benita beamed. "I was only doing my civic duty."

After the police went over my statement, they said they would increase the number of patrol cars in the area. Ms. Benita showed them out and then stayed with me until Detective Harris arrived. When Detective Harris arrived, I introduced him to Ms. Benita and he thanked her for being there for me. Again, Ms. Benita said she was only doing what a good neighbor would do. I tried smiling, but couldn't. She turned to me and asked whether I wanted her to stay with me. Before I could reply, Detective Harris pulled her to the side and whispered something in her ear. She winked at me and said she would check in on me tomorrow. This time I managed to smile and told her I would like that.

Detective Harris sat beside me on the sofa and told me that he was deeply concerned about what happened. He wanted me to start from the beginning and not leave any detail out, no matter how small or insignificant. I was already exhausted after talking to the police, but I knew with his relentless questioning, I had no choice but to recount the entire incident step by step when all I wanted him to do was hug me and possibly spend the night. Maybe I was just feeling emotionally exposed or he represented something I hadn't had in a while, security.

Folding his arms, he sank back into the sofa and listened intently. He kept nodding his head as if processing each piece of information. "You said you received a threatening text message. Show me."

"Yes, here it is." I gave him my cell phone. "It's from a blocked number."

He read it and a worried look crossed his face. "I'm going to stay here with you tonight."

"I, uh—"

He raised his hand to shut me up. "You don't always have to be tough. It's okay to need someone."

"Well, I..."

"Deidre, this is getting really dangerous. You need to change your phone number to avoid getting more text messages like this."

"I'm not scared. They already know where I live, besides it would take me forever to call everyone and tell them I have a new number."

I knew that Detective Harris wanted to protect me and I felt good that he did. But I would be damned if I let anyone scare me without knowing the reason why. Kyle was always on the go and I had no choice but to take care of everything that needed fixing around the house including maintenance on my car, paying all the bills and after a while, I felt it was pointless having a man around who claimed to be my husband. Kyle was clueless and he didn't realize that all the material things didn't mean much to me and I would give them all up just for him to be present. So, for once it felt good to feel protected and I relinquished my independence that night and fell asleep in Detective Harris's arms.

CHAPTER 7

WHEN I WOKE UP THE next morning, I found a note Detective Harris had left for me on the coffee table. I smiled as I read it out loud:

"Dear Deidre, I watched you sleep and you looked so peaceful. Please get some rest. Will call you later—H."

That was such a sweet gesture on his part and made me want to get to know the sensitive side of this man. I yawned, folded the note, placed it on the table and went back to sleep on the sofa.

At 11:45 a.m. I got up, took a shower and put on some lounge-wear. I still ached from the bruises and had no plans to leave the house. Thirty minutes later, Ms. Benita was ringing my doorbell to check on me as promised. This afternoon I didn't mind the interruption. I stepped aside to let her in as she handed me a basket filled with freshly baked blueberry muffins.

"Mmmm, Ms. Benita, you know how much I love your muffins," I said, reaching for one.

"I knew they would cheer you up a bit, but chile can't you wait until we get to the kitchen?"

"Sorry, where are my manners?"

"But seriously, how ya feeling today? Did you get some rest?" Ms. Benita asked, making her way to the kitchen table. She pulled out a chair, sat down and took out a muffin.

"Hold on, let me get you a plate." I opened the overhead cabinet and pulled out two plates and two mugs. "Coffee?"

"Sure."

"I hope you're not in a hurry. Um, I'd really like the company." I poured the coffee and offered Ms. Benita some cream and sugar.

Stirring her coffee, she said, "Chile, what else do I have to do other than spy on the neighbors?"

I laughed and nodded in agreement.

"So, that's your detective friend, huh? He sure is handsome. Hmm, if I was only twenty years younger, I would give you a run for your money."

"Now, Ms. Benita, you know you are so wrong. But he sure is fine." I beamed.

Ms. Benita spent an hour with me gossiping about the neighbors as we drank more coffee and ate the last two muffins.

"Well, I have to get going if I want to catch the Flea Market before they close," she said, rising from her chair and dusting off some crumbs from her sweater. "Gotta see what knick knacks they have on sale."

"You're such a collector," I said.

Ms. Benita laughed as she leaned in to give me a hug.

"Thanks for checking in on me. I'll walk you to the door."

"You can't be too careful these days. I have an extra baseball bat if you want it," Ms. Benita said.

"I'm good but thanks." I locked the door and watched Ms. Benita get into her station wagon and pull out of her driveway.

An hour later, I called Kyle to tell him about last night's incident. He remained quiet while I related the details and then he reamed into me for not being more careful. I listened for a minute and then hung up in his ears. He tried calling me back several times, but I let the calls go directly to voicemail.

So much for empathy, I thought.

I was still aching and there was no way I could perform at the Kitty Kat Club on Sunday. My back was up against the wall and I didn't want to lose precious time in getting information. I had a feeling that Trixie could be trusted, so I took a chance, picked up the phone and called Frederick's of Hollywood. I hoped she was working and that she wouldn't hang up on me when she heard my proposal for her filling in for me at the club because I had no other options. After I explained everything about the shooting and that I was going undercover to do my own investigation, but I had been hurt, she agreed.

"Okay, I'll cover for you and let you know what I find out," Trixie said.

"Thanks, girl. I know this is a lot to ask, but be careful," I said.

"I will. I'm from the streets of Philly so I can handle mine," Trixie said, reassuring me.

"I hear ya." I disconnected the call and then conjured up my street voice to make the next call to Marvin. He answered after four rings sounding out of breath.

"Yeeeah, who dis?"

"Hey, it's Private Dancer. You busy?"

"Nah, wassup?"

"I can't make it tomorrow. I'm not feeling well, lower back pain."

Marvin sucked his teeth. "Damn, so what? I'm out a dancer? Where the hell..."

"Hey, hey, I got you. My girl, Trixie can fill in for me. Can I give her your digits?"

"Man, aight. Tell her I'ma wait for her call later and she betta be ready to come to da club 'round four this evening to show me if she can work that thang."

"Cool. I'll give my girl the heads up. Sorry Marvin, I,..."

Click. Marvin was so abrupt, but I guess in his line of business that was acceptable.

Trixie called me later that evening and told me all about her audition at the club and that Marvin was all up in her face. She told me he liked her dancing style and was impressed that she had danced before. Guess he saw dollar signs once he laid eyes on her curvaceous body and her smooth mocha skin. Needless to say, Trixie got the job and started the following night at nine. She still needed protection and with what just happened to me, I needed Marcusetta to have Cassius keep an eye on the situation in case it turned ugly.

I had been away from my antique shop, Trinkets & Art Delights, since Lia's death. Although I left Tori in charge and she gave me frequent updates via e-mail I still missed dealing with the customers. Driving through the streets of Georgetown toward the shop, I marveled at all the new developments throughout the years: trendy shops, restaurants, and bars. When the Waterfront Park opened not too long ago, I had planned for Lia and me to spend a Saturday afternoon shopping and then walking along the promenade overlooking the Potomac River, but we never got around to coordinating our schedules. I felt a twinge of sadness.

It was ten o'clock in the morning and the shop already had a few customers browsing around looking at various items on sale. Tori greeted me with a warm hug and her smiling green eyes and gave me the mail from the past couple of days. She knew well not to bug me about her design ideas for some new line of lamps we were set to carry in the spring. I went to my office and sat in front of my computer and sifted through the bills. My daily routine had to go on except for a few bumps in the road like being attacked a few days ago. I was still scared, but I was happy that Detective Harris checked on me frequently. I was beginning to warm to the idea of us getting closer, but my divorce was still not finalized. Since Kyle got out of the hospital he had been traveling out of state for business and our attorneys couldn't coordinate a mutually agreeable time for all parties to meet after the shooting incident.

I hated when things dragged out. If I were a betting woman I would suspect that Kyle had something to do with the delay just so he could attempt to change my mind. I stared out my window and thought how he tried to ambush me into reconsidering the divorce after the shooting.

This happened the day he was discharged from the hospital when he took me out to dinner at a seafood restaurant in Fell's Point to thank me for taking care of him. After the second glass of wine, he asked me to withdraw the divorce because his accountant said it was just bad timing for me to get a divorce in the midst of preparing the company's tax records. It was just like him to have the gall to make this demand. I laughed and almost threw the glass of wine in his face, but I restrained myself from causing a scene. Instead, I politely thanked him for the meal, walked out and hailed a cab back to his townhouse to pick up my car.

A knock on my door startled me. "Come in."

Tori entered my office hidden behind a huge bouquet of a dozen red roses.

"For me?"

"Yes, so who's the admirer?" Tori placed the vase on my desk and stood there waiting for me to read the card.

"Ah, I won't disclose," I said coyly, putting my hand up against my ear. "Is that the door chime, I hear? I think a customer just walked in."

Tori laughed. "Well, it won't be a secret for too long."

I read the card. "*Just because. Love you still. Kyle.*"

He never gives up. Always the perfect gentleman whenever he needed to win you over. Not this time. Lia's death shook me to my core and made me re-evaluate all my relationships and treasure every special moment. But my moment with Kyle had come and gone and I was now ready to be single again without the drama of constant infidelity and scams that almost cost me everything but my underwear.

It was lunch time and I found a few carry-out menus in my desk drawer and settled on ordering Chinese for everyone. I ate at my desk and remained there for the majority of the day, checking and sending e-mails and fielding calls from potential clients for more of my high-end antique furniture. At around six o'clock, I was beat and ready to head home. Tori said she would lock up and that I shouldn't worry. Grabbing my handbag, I walked to the parking lot around the corner to get my car.

When I got close enough to my car, I saw a piece of paper under my windshield. My heart raced. I stopped for a few seconds and swallowed the lump in my throat. Nervously, I reached into my bag and pulled out my mace. I steadied my hands. This time, I was ready in case something was about to jump off. I straightened my back and bravely walked up to my car expecting a threatening note, but to my relief it was a flyer advertising the opening of a new sub shop a few blocks down from my store. I exhaled, unlocked the car doors, slid behind the wheel and pulled into traffic.

On my ride home, a call from Detective Harris beeped into the end of a voicemail message I was leaving for Angela. I quickly finished up the message and clicked over to answer his call.

"Hey, Hill. What's up?"

"Just touching base with you."

"Did you guys find LaTasha yet?"

"No, can't seem to locate her."

"What about the license plate number Ms. Benita gave the police?" I asked.

"That was a dead end. The plates were from a stolen vehicle from New Jersey."

"Hmm, clever," I said quietly.

"What did you say?"

"Um, nothing." I sighed. *I guess we're not messing with amateurs.*

"Deidre, you there?"

"Yes. Hill, let me call you back. I gotta concentrate on getting home." Those were the last words I said before noticing a multiple car accident ahead of me causing a pile up and the endless traffic I was stuck in for hours. Fighting fatigue, I finally made it home at 9 p.m. Again, I made sure to have my mace and keys in hand before scanning the area and rushing into my house.

CHAPTER 8

TRIXIE HAD BEEN DANCING AT the Kitty Kat Club for a few days and reported nothing out of the ordinary, until 2 a.m. Thursday morning. I was feeling a little better except for a few minor aches and pains which forced me to go to bed early. The sound of my cell phone ringing startled me, almost causing me to knock over the lamp scrambling to answer the call.

"This better be good," I grumbled.

"Oh, hey, Deidre. Didn't mean to call you so late but I just couldn't wait."

"Mmm–hmm." I put the phone on speaker.

"Girl, Cassius is such a cool dude. He doesn't mind waiting for me when I dance really late. I really like him, he's so cool—"

"Trixie, focus. Skip to the part where you tell me why you're calling."

"Sorry, girl. Well, LaTasha showed up at the club and danced a couple of sets."

"Uh-huh."

"And then a detective guy showed up and pulled her to the side. I couldn't hear what they were saying, so I got closer to ear hustle."

I laughed. "I see you've been hanging with Cassius quite a bit."

"Yeah, a little." Trixie chuckled. "I'm trying to stay focused here. Anyway, I heard the detective say to LaTasha that she needed to come down to the police station with him to answer some questions. All of a sudden, LaTasha flipped out and started waving her hands around and raising her voice. It didn't take long for folks to start staring."

"What did the detective do?"

"He was calm and when she saw he wasn't buying into her craziness, she chilled out and then went with him."

Yeah, that's Hill, so diplomatic, I thought.

"Deidre, you still listening?"

"Ah, yeah. What else?"

"Oh and when she got her coat and was leaving the club, she started flirting with him, twirling the curls in her weave, and pushing her titties up in his face."

"And then what happened?" I sat up, waiting to hear her response.

"He ignored her again, like she wasn't even there. She's such a trick."

I laughed. "We still have a lot of unanswered questions though."

"I know, but that information was still good, right?"

"Yes, thanks Trixie. Oh, hey, try to get close to LaTasha, try to make her trust you."

"Okay, that shouldn't be too hard. She thinks she's in charge around here and likes giving orders and advice."

I heard a whistle on the other end of the phone. "Who's that?"

"It's Cassius, telling me to hurry up. It's cold out here, so I better get my butt to the car."

"Well, good night, Trixie."

"Sorry again for calling so late, but I couldn't wait."

"No worries. Get home safe and don't do anything I wouldn't do."

"Right, whatever you say," Trixie said, laughing before she hung up.

I turned off my phone, fixed my pink satin cap on my head, fluffed up my pillow, rolled onto my side and went back to sleep.

The sun's rays gently eased in through the blinds and rested on the side of my face. I turned and looked at the clock on the nightstand and noticed it was 11 a.m. I did a total body stretch before kicking the covers to the floor and then hopping into the shower. I had to get ready and meet Angela for our girls' spa day including lunch, which I desperately needed after the attack.

I was standing in front of the mirror in the bathroom, applying some lip gloss and putting the finishing touches to my hair, when Angela called. "Hey girl, just checking to make sure we're still on for today."

"Yup, thanks for making the appointments. I really need a good massage and some pampering today."

"Me too girl. My hips still hurt from doing all that climbing on the Stairmaster."

"See, that's why I don't even fool with that machine," I said.

"Okay, get a move on, you know where the spa is, right?"

"I got my handy navigation system, so hopefully I shouldn't get lost. See ya in a few."

I was glad Angela was no longer angry with me for hiding the details about Lia's murder. She thought we were much closer as friends and I should have trusted her. She was right and despite apologizing for days, she didn't take my calls until after Lia's funeral because I really needed a sympathetic ear. Now that Lia was gone, Angela was the only trusted friend I had left.

An hour later, we were dressed in spa robes and slippers. The staff told us to wait in the lounge area and to enjoy the complimentary refreshments before the masseuse came to get us. I looked around the room and admired the walls painted in the softest shades of blue, green and beige. I sat back and inhaled the scented candles and relaxed to the sounds of the ocean piping through the in-ceiling speakers.

Despite the good time I was having, my mind shifted to a call I got yesterday from the receptionist at the Law Offices of Hardwick and Knox, reminding me about the settlement conference tomorrow to sign the divorce papers. That put a damper on my mood until Angela's voice came into focus.

"Yeah girl, did you see *Real Housewives of Atlanta?*"

"Ah, no. I'm too busy dealing with my own issues."

"Well, you know I'm a reality show nut," she said laughing.

She was ready to tell me all about the drama before I cut her off.

Driving home after lunch, I clicked on my Bluetooth and checked my voicemail. There was one marked urgent from Hill.

"Hey Deidre, it's Hill. Just wanted to let you know I tracked down LaTasha last night at the Kitty Kat Club. She put up some resistance but she eventually came down to the station for questioning. She said she heard the shots and panicked and then threw her wig in the dumpster for fear that the police would pick her up as a witness. Hey, get this, she said she was wearing that outfit and wig because a co-worker dared her to do it for one hundred bucks."

I heard a pause and then a sarcastic chuckle from Hill.

"I had to let her go because there was no solid evidence to hold her as a suspect, but I think she's hiding something. I just can't seem to put my finger on it."

I clicked off my Bluetooth and wondered why he didn't mention anything about the file from the State's Attorney's Office. This was driving me crazy and so I called in a favor.

"Hey girl," Gina said.

"They working you in the dungeon?" I asked, fidgeting with the radio in my car.

"Yeah. I can't even complain with the economy in half, I'm lucky to have a job. Anyway, what you want?"

"I need a little favor, can you hook your cousin up?"

"Girl, you betta not get me fired!" she quipped jokingly.

"I promise, I won't cost you your J.O.B. I need you to pull the Taevon Jackson file for me."

"Damn, girl. I thought you quit that fighting crime bullshit. Okay, I'll see what I can find. Let me put you on hold."

"Thanks a bunch."

A few minutes went by before Gina came back and interrupted the elevator music that was playing in my ear. "Deidre, I got the file right here. What you wanna know?"

"I need you to verify that Lia Reynolds was on the witness list."

"Yup, she was on the list."

"What can you tell me about Taevon's priors?"

"You know you can just come down here and review the file yourself. Ah, yeah, too busy running some fancy antique shop where regular folks can't afford to buy anything."

"You know I don't feel like seeing a lot of folks asking me questions and getting all up in my business if I come there."

"Well, the file says Taevon Jackson is a local thug wannabe. Damn, he's just twenty-one. He barely got titty milk off his breath, just a baby. What's wrong with our youth of today?"

"Hold on, let me pull into this gas station," I said.

"You betta hurry up."

I quickly turned into the gas station and parked next to the vacuum machine. I pulled out a notepad that I kept under the passenger seat for occasions just like this. Gina was reading off Taevon's priors and I was quickly jotting down notes to compare with Hill during our upcoming conversation about the file.

"This dude is no joke. Don't know what you're doing but be careful."

"I will and thanks, you're a doll."

Gina whispered, "Yeah, yeah, I gotta get off this phone, boss man's coming and you know I can't stand his ass."

When the call ended, I reviewed the notes and was happy with the information that she had given me. Now all I needed was to find a connection between Taevon Jackson and Lia's murder.

Later that evening, I had a stack of paper full of notes about Taevon Jackson and his crew after searching the Maryland court records and newspaper databases. I learned that he had been in and out of the juvenile court system for various offenses. He was no stranger to the courts and it was only a matter of time before his crimes escalated to murder. He was the leader of a drug crew that was known for initiations including brutal beatings, muggings and car jackings. I guess he wanted to teach his crew of ten strong and growing how to handle anything that got in their way of building his empire.

I shook my head and wondered what went wrong in the households of these young men to make them want to be locked down in a 6-by-8-feet cell where they could hardly breathe. I had read enough and now my eyes were tired. I needed to rest up so I could finally close the chapter on Kyle.

CHAPTER 9

I ARRIVED AT THE LAW OFFICES of Hardwick and Knox at 9 a.m. and waited for Kyle to make his grand entrance. When he did, he walked in with his head hanging down. I was sad too as this was the end of an era.

"Hey, Deidre. How ya doing? I didn't mean to snap at you the other day when you called and told me about the attack."

"Right, but it's all good now."

"Is it? I won't have you to keep me straight, you know you're my anchor," he said, looking at me with sad puppy eyes.

"Kyle, don't do this. Not now."

He sat down next to me in the receptionist's area and tried holding my hand. He was about to say something when the receptionist motioned for us to enter the conference room.

Whew, that was close. I got up and headed to the conference room with Kyle at my heels.

A few hours later, with the divorce settlement papers signed and the final hearing of the matter at the Circuit Court for Baltimore City, the reality kicked in that I had to get used to being single again. I convinced myself it shouldn't be too hard since I often felt single in a marriage where I was the only participant. Kyle was an absentee, skirt chasing husband who paraded around town driving in his BMW convertible looking for his next piece of 'entertainment.' Like most men, the head between his ears went blank when new pussy came around, especially the ones that needed to be rescued.

I guess I had outgrown my usefulness and was too strong for the likes of him. So I got kicked to the curb once he started his pussy rescue mission. What Kyle failed to realize was that he was pushing thirty-five and his playboy days were coming to an end; I just hoped he would not come running back for me to fix him.

Once I got home, I didn't want to wallow in self-pity and I needed to get a boost. I called Angela to tell her about the divorce.

"Girl, don't even sweat it."

I remained silent.

"You're better off without him. You're a strong sister, you'll be okay." "Mmm-hmm."

"You know what would perk you up?" Angela asked mischievously.

"What? A bottle of wine and some—"

"Just be ready to go at six, we're going to a spoken word club in D.C."

It took nothing but a second for my eyes to light up and agree to the suggestion. I loved poetry and every now and then I would dabble by writing a few words which I kept in my personal diary. This was a great way to celebrate my single-hood and I needed my outfit to make such a statement without looking like a hoochie.

At six o'clock sharp, Angela arrived dressed in a pair of skinny jeans, a sheer silver top and high heels. When I climbed into the car, I threw my coat on top of hers in the back seat. She turned on the radio and started singing along and snapping her fingers to the music all the way to the poetry club. We circled the block a couple of times before we found parking two blocks away and hurriedly walked to the club.

"Hurry up, we have to get in early to get a good seat before the show starts," she said as she strutted ahead of me.

"I'm walking as fast as I can. Damn, I almost tripped," I said, trying to steady myself.

"No one told you to wear them high heeled boots, trying to look cute," she said snickering.

"I'll be okay, once I get on the sidewalk," I laughed, tightening my scarf around my neck.

It was now seven o'clock and there was a line waiting outside the door to get in. I was shivering from the cold and although I had my gloves on, I kept rubbing my hands together for extra warmth. When we finally got into the club I was surprised that it had an art gallery, a bar, a bookstore, and a restaurant. We wanted to grab a bite to eat before the show began so we placed our names on the waiting list. I then decided to peruse the bookstore until they called us.

Angela went to the aisle with the gossip magazines. She was shaking her head as she flipped through the pages of *Star* magazine. I went to the fiction section and got excited when I found a newly released novel by Eric Jerome Dickey, one of my favorite authors. I paid for my book just in time as the hostess called our names. The place was packed with eclectic, afro-centric authors, writers, Howard University students, couples on first dates and then there was me, a newly divorcee. I doubt if anyone cared, but I blended right in with the crowd wearing my leather jacket, black slacks, off-white V-neck sweater, silver accessories, high-heeled boots and soft curls all over my head.

We squeezed in between two couples to get to our table with barely enough room to hold two plates and two drinks. I ordered a spinach and wheat berry salad because I didn't have much of an appetite and Angela ordered the catfish dinner.

"Girl, I've been running around all day doing errands. I need me some real food, can't do any lettuce eating tonight," Angela said.

"I may want to have some dessert so the salad should be good for now," I said, spearing a piece of lettuce into my mouth.

We finished our meals and waited for the show to start at eight. By this time, I was on my second cup of cappuccino and Angela was busy looking around at folks and talking trash about them. I didn't feel much like people watching and anxiously waited for the poet-in-residence to announce the lineup of poets.

The first poet stepped to the stage and rocked the house with his in your face words about issues of love and race. I felt challenged and enlightened by his words and wanted more.

Angela stood up and shouted, "Yeah, that's right brother!"

After the first round of poets took a break, the musicians were introduced to the crowd. When the poet-in-residence announced Hill Harris on drums, I almost spit my cappuccino across the room.

"Girl, what's wrong with you?" Angela asked with a baffled look on her face.

I wiped my mouth with a napkin and stammered. "That's the...uh, uh." I pointed toward the stage. "The detective guy I was telling you about."

Angela eyed me suspiciously. "Oh, oooh, the one I know you are feeling but won't admit to it?" She craned her neck forward to get a good look at him which she couldn't because we were almost in the back of the room. Suddenly, she jumped up.

"Angela, where are you going?"

"I gotta get a good look at this man," Angela said, taking off toward the stage.

I tried reaching for her, but she was too fast.

Dear God. What is she going to do?

I sat there watching her as she made her way through the crowded room to the stage and motioned to Hill. He bent down to hear what she had to say. He stood up and looked into the crowd, but the lights were too dim. Angela came back to the table and sat in her seat with a big smile on her face.

"What on earth did you say to him, are you crazy?"

Angela smiled devilishly. "You'll see." She picked up her hot chocolate which was now cold, took a sip and got ready for the second half of the show.

The performances in the second half of the show were great as each poet brought their 'A' game. When the last act of the night was about to perform, Angela got up to go to the ladies' room. I noticed she had been gone for more than five minutes before she called my cell phone. The room was noisy with all the chatter from the patrons so I had to cover my right ear to hear her.

I shouted, "Angela, what's taking you so long?"

"I gotta go girl, that Hill guy said he would take you home."

"What the..."

"I know, I know, girl, yeah, you gonna whoop my ass." Angela laughed.

"You think this is funny?"

"You gotta be spontaneous. What do I keep telling you?"

"Oh, I see. So this is your way of daring me to be spontaneous by going home with this man."

"You'll be fine. Maybe you need him tonight. If you know what I mean," Angela said laughing.

"You're such a comedian," I said sarcastically.

Detective Harris appeared before me and interrupted the call and I hung up on Angela.

Spontaneity here I come. I dabbed my mouth with a napkin and extended my hand to him which he took with such grace, easing me out of my seat that I almost melted.

"Well, this is quite a surprise. Who knew you liked poetry," he said.

There's a lot you don't know about me, I thought.

"Um, your friend Angela said you'd be needing a ride home?" he asked.

"Ah, yeah. If you don't mind. Would cost me a grip to call a cab." I was seething. *I'm going to KILL her.*

"Wait out front while I go get the car. Gimmie about five minutes."

"No problem. I gotta take care of the bill." *Oh, I'm so going to KILL her.*

After paying the bill, I put my jacket on, picked up my book, walked to the door, pressed my face up against the glass and waited anxiously for Hill to drive up. When he did, all eyes followed me to the car. I guess he must be popular at this place.

The ride home was pleasant. While Hill was bringing me up-to-date on the case, I made sure to hide the fact that I had Trixie working at the club and spying on LaTasha. When he finally pulled up in my driveway, I didn't want the conversation to end. So I asked him to come in for a night cap and he didn't hesitate.

He took off his coat and made himself comfortable on the sofa. I got us two wine glasses and a bottle of Chardonnay that I had chilling in the fridge to do my own celebrating, but now the more the merrier. Several glasses of wine later, Hill lifted up my chin and said in the most seductive voice, "I want to kiss you."

I threw caution to the wind and kissed him back. His lips were so soft and inviting to my tongue. His hands touched the small of my back and I quivered. The door to the Y was coming open with each kiss he gave me. I pulled him on top of me and laid back on the sofa. My legs opened to accommodate his weight. I could feel his breath on my neck and I let out a moan that had been locked up for too long.

"Hill, I don't know if I can do this," I said softly.

He whispered, "Yes, you can, Deidre. You gotta let it go, trust me baby."

He went to unbutton my slacks and I stopped him. "Hill, not like this."

"Okay then. I'll stop. Guess we're moving too fast."

"Mmm-hmm." I moaned.

He got up off of me and sat up.

I fixed my sweater and let out a deep breath. *Damn, I want this man, but I don't think I'm ready yet.*

"Hey, it's getting late. I better be going," he said.

"Um, yeah. Thanks for the ride home."

"Girl, you are such a temptress. But hey, I understand. Maybe next time." He placed his hands on his knees and rose from the sofa. He grabbed his coat and his keys and headed to the front door. Turning around, he said with concern in his voice, "Will you be okay? I know your divorce was finalized today."

That damn Angela. I guess she felt I needed some loving tonight. I managed a smile and said, "I'm fine."

He gave me a hug and before leaving he made a motion to the alarm, reminding me to put it on. I pulled back the curtain and watched him get into his car. As I was about to close the curtains, I saw Ms. Benita's porch light come on. I quickly hit the light switch on the wall and peered through the peephole.

What I saw next surprised me and made me smile. Larry, my neighbor who was always washing his "fleet" of cars was leaving Ms. Benita's house. I saw her plant a big kiss on his cheek and then Larry pulled her closer to him for another kiss, this time on her lips. Ms. Benita was getting her groove on and here I am turning down a perfect ending to a rather jacked-up day of events.

Oh, well, can't say I'm mad at her.

CHAPTER 10

ONE OF THE DREADED THINGS about Fall is raking the never ending leaves in your yard. I didn't mind it though, as it allowed me to get some fresh air and catch up with some of my neighbors who were outside tackling the same task. After I bagged up the first round of leaves and was putting it at the curb, I looked up and saw Ms. Benita coming out of her front door. She was wearing a pair of work gloves and ready to do some yard work. I waved to her and she returned a big cheesy smile. I grinned back, knowing of her late night tryst with Larry.

I turned up the volume on my iPod and starting bopping to my music while I worked. As I stopped to take a sip from my bottled water, Hill appeared out of the corner of my eye. I wanted to run inside to freshen up, but it would look too obvious so I just stood there and held onto the rake in front of me.

"Hey, Deidre, got a minute?" he asked, poking his head out the window.

I threw the rake in the grass, unplugged my earphones and walked over to his car.

"Checking in on me?"

"Yeah, making sure we're still cool."

"Sure." I thought, *why wouldn't we be?*

"Hop in."

"Huh, I look like a bum and my hair is a mess."

"Don't matter," he said.

"No, just come on inside. Pleeease," I pleaded, clasping my hands together.

"Well, all right then."

I pointed to my car in the driveway. "Park behind me and come on in." Wiping my hands on the front of my jeans, I headed inside the house. I left the front door unlocked and quickly rifled through the laundry basket sitting at the bottom of the stairs and found a clean shirt to change into. Hill came into the living room sniffling and sat on the sofa.

"Catching a cold, are we?" I handed him a box of Kleenex as I sat down next to him.

"Thanks." He blew his nose, balled it up and threw it into the waste basket across the room.

"That's a three pointer. You should've been a basketball player." I clapped. "What's up?"

"I finally got a hold of the case file and talked to the prosecutor handling it. We're chasing down some leads."

Sitting closer to the edge of the sofa, I had my attention deeply fixed on him. "Yeah, go on," I said.

"Seems like Taevon is a drug dealer wannabe with a growing crew of young thugs."

"How did Lia get caught up in this?" I asked as if I didn't already know that she was scheduled to testify against Taevon.

"Wrong place, wrong time. She was going into the store to buy some orange juice when Taevon came rushing out, almost knocking her down. She got a good look at his face and when she went into the store she found the store owner with two gunshot wounds to the head."

I shook my head. "It's just like Lia to do the right thing, coming forward to the police about this shooting. And look what it cost her...her life." I held back a tear as my voice began to crack.

"Yeah," he said, shaking his head.

"Does Taevon have any priors?"

"More than enough for his twenty-one years," he responded.

"I'm amazed how many of these young men choose the path filled with horror. I bet Taevon thinks he's invincible."

"He and so many others think they wear an S on their chest. I wouldn't be surprised if he's connected somehow to your attack and the message you got on your cell phone."

That thought scared me as I didn't know how far Taevon's reach was on the street although he was locked up. Too bad kryptonite wasn't sold in stores. "What now?"

"Right now, we have surveillance on the entire crew," Hill said.

"That's good." I felt confident that the police were taking swift action.

"We're being very careful not to blow this case. We're gonna have to try to catch them doing something criminal and maybe have them turn on Taevon. We'll see."

"I'm glad you're working this case." I reached over and lightly stroked his hand. I was really getting used to seeing Hill, and even though it was case related, I wouldn't mind seeing him when he had some down time and all this was over.

Hill's cell phone rang and he looked at the number and frowned. He raised his finger at me and said, "Give me a second. I have to take this."

He got up and walked toward the kitchen before he answered.

I was curious to know what was going on, so I got up pretending to go to the guest powder room near the kitchen but left the door slightly open so I could eavesdrop on the conversation. I could only hear bits and pieces because he was whispering.

"Yeah, this is Harris. What? No...When?...That motherfucker... Damn it!" He ended the call.

I flushed the toilet, turned on the faucet and pretended to wash my hands. When I opened the door, I almost bumped into him heading into the living room. His whole demeanor had changed from being relaxed and talkative to tense and abrupt. I took this as a sign that whoever was on the other end of the line didn't have good news to share with him. I approached him cautiously.

"What do ya have planned for the day?" I tried easing the tension in the room.

"Not much. Look Deidre, something came up and I really must go," he said in a straightforward manner.

"I understand. I'm here if you need to talk about anything other than the case. I mean it."

"Thanks. That's good to know," he said, buttoning up his coat. He gave me a longing look and headed for the front door. Shortly after he left, the doorbell rang and I thought he had forgotten something. I rushed to answer it and to my surprise it was Angela.

"Oh, hey, girl. What you doing out here in my neighborhood? Trying to get the scoop on last night. You know I'm mad at you." I gave her a hug and pulled her inside.

"Yup, I know. Just saw lover boy Hill leaving. He didn't look too happy. I guess he didn't get any last night?"

"It wasn't even like that. I chickened out and he left. He just stopped by to talk about the case."

"How's it going?" Angela asked, taking off her coat and putting it on a hanger in the closet near the front door.

"Well, he has the case file and ah..." I paused. "The guy on the murder rap is only twenty-one and a gang leader. I hate to think that he had his boys kill Lia so he could beat the charges." I shook my head in disbelief, but the reality was that this type of thing happened every now and then unless the State had other evidence to put these criminals away.

"These young men today don't care. It's the gangsta mentality. But don't worry, he's gonna get what's coming to him sooner rather than later. You'll see. God works in mysterious ways," Angela said.

"Amen to that!" I raised my hands to the heavens and hoped it was true.

After Angela left, I cross-referenced my notes with the information Hill shared with me before rushing out in such a hurry. All the information checked out, but I was puzzled as to his sudden departure. I went to my study and fired up the computer. While it was booting up I went to the kitchen and filled a bowl with Chex party mix and grabbed a soda from the fridge. The house phone rang just as I was putting a handful of pretzels and bagel chips in my mouth. I was still chewing when I answered the phone.

"Deidre?"

I finished chewing and took a sip of my soda. "Yeah Tori, how's everything going at the shop?"

"Great! We had a mad rush for those jewelry boxes with the personal notes inside of them. Who knew they would be such hot sellers?"

"I told you they would be a hit. So what can't you find in my office today?"

"Nothing. I was wondering if I could close a little early today. Gotta pick up my car from the body shop before they close."

"Sure. Did you make today's deposit?"

"Yep."

"Great, make sure they don't rip you off at the body shop."

"I got Rod with me."

"Called in your big brother, huh? They better not mess with you now."

"Yeah. See ya soon?"

I sighed. "I plan to come in over the weekend and make a few display changes. Guess I'll see you on Monday."

"Take care and enjoy your weekend," Tori said in a bubbly manner.

"You do the same." I hung up the phone and logged into my e-mail account.

After deleting several discount offers from various department stores, my curiosity about Hill took a hold of me and I Googled his name. I found seven hits but narrowed the search down to those in Brooklyn, New York. When I clicked on his name, I found several newspaper articles about his wife's murder with graphic details. She was a beautiful woman who was on the brink of launching her own line of handbags and accessories. There were pictures of both of them volunteering at a rebuilding project in the neighborhood and they looked so happy together two weeks prior to her death.

I kept reading and found a few other articles that described the "Moonlight Strangler" as a ghost that "almost wrecked an exemplary detective's career." I continued reading and learned that Hill went to New York University, graduated top of his class at the police academy and quickly ascended to the ranks of detective. The more I read about him, the more intrigued I became and wanted to get to know this man. I couldn't imagine what he must have gone through after his wife's death and still have the will to go on, knowing that the killer was out there. All this research wore me out and I powered down the computer and headed to my bedroom.

I was about to charge up my cell phone when I saw a call coming in from Trixie. I laughed out loud thinking that my house had become call central.

"Hey Trixie, what's up?"

"I can't talk too long," she whispered. "I'm here at a bachelor party and LaTasha is really showing her ass."

"What do you mean? What's she doing?"

"She's all over these men and wants to sleep with the groom. She's drunk as hell and some guy who brought us here is mugging like crazy. He doesn't say much and has a big scar on his neck. When he got out the car he was limping and just now when he sat down, I saw a gun strapped to his ankle. I'm kinda scared."

"Calm down. Are they forcing you to do things you don't want to do?" I asked, concerned for her safety.

"No. LaTasha told them up front that I don't roll like that."

"Good. Where is Cassius?"

"He's sick as a dog. But said he'd come get me if they started tripping."

Damn. What did I get her into?

Then I heard a female voice in the background shouting. "Hey Trixie, who ya talking to? The fellas need you to dance for them one more time. Whoo, hoo. Dat's my song, crank it up!"

"Coming girl," Trixie said, before the phone went dead.

I held the phone in my hand and wondered whether I had a handle on the situation. I didn't want to put Trixie in harm's way, but felt secure that she would call Cassius to get her if things began to get out of hand.

When I finally made it to bed, I kept tossing and turning, wondering whether the guy Trixie described to me was the same guy I prosecuted for drugs years ago. How coincidental that he was limping—could it be from a leg wound? If this was the same person then I may have also found my attacker. But the million dollar question still remained, how was he connected to LaTasha and how was she involved in Lia's death?

CHAPTER 11

I CAME BACK FROM JOGGING AROUND the neighborhood and stopped for a brief moment to catch my breath in the driveway. I bent over and rested my hands on my knees and then wiped the sweat from my brow with the back of my hand. I had left my cell phone in the house and heard it ringing when I opened the front door. I rushed over to the kitchen counter to answer it.

"Hello," I said, trying to catch my breath.

"Deidre, you all right?" Hill asked.

"Yup, yeah, just went jogging. Where are you?" I could hear noise in the background, cars honking, and people yelling. I shouted, "Hill, I can't hear you. Where are you?"

"In New York," he shouted back.

"Why?" I shouted again.

"Hold on."

The noise in the background subsided and I could hear him more clearly now.

"Yeah, a buddy of mine from the precinct I worked at in Brooklyn called me yesterday and said they may have caught the 'Moonlight Strangler.'"

"Is that why you left in such a hurry yesterday?" I pried.

"Sorry about that. I didn't want to get into it and had to rush home to pack a few things before I got on the road."

"Is it really the Moonlight Strangler?"

"Hmm, I don't know. He's not talking and lawyered up." Hill let out a sigh. "I wish I could hurt him, the way he hurt Sierra."

I could hear the venom in his voice.

"I know how you feel." I paused. "Hill, listen to me. Whatever you decide, it's not worth you losing your job or risking going to jail. Sierra's gone and there's nothing you can do to bring her back."

"It's just..." he paused. "If that son of a bitch walk away from this..."

"I know, but you need to think clearly and let the system work for you."

"This is true. Are you always this rational?" he asked in a calmer voice.

"No, not always. But I would hate for a good brother like you to be on lock down." I thought, *he has no idea how irrational I can be at times.*

"True." He managed to laugh.

"Hey, remember you're building a new life and making new friends who care about you here in Maryland," I said light-heartedly.

"Thanks, Deidre. That means a lot."

I heard someone shout, "Yo, Hill wassup son?"

"Go handle your business and let me know when you get back into town."

"Cool." Before the call disconnected I heard him say, "Hey, man, haven't seen you in a minute. Wassup?"

Later that evening, I was watching the six o'clock news when I saw that the police had made a major drug bust in East Baltimore. Large quantities of drugs and firearms were seized and arrests were made. The camera shifted to four young men. They were hand-cuffed and three hung their heads low, but there was one who stared directly into the camera. He showed no fear and his piercing eyes were full of hatred and contempt. I almost jumped out of my skin when I saw the scar on the side of his neck and realized that he was the same guy who threatened me years ago. He walked with a slight limp on his left side and I shuddered to think that I had come face to face with my attacker on the TV. I needed to find out more specific details about the arrest, but I had to wait until Hill got back to town.

I had no plans to go out so I decided to make some pasta, drink some wine and catch up on some reading. While the pasta was cooking I called Trixie to see how she made out at the bachelor party. I had meant to call her earlier, but I got sidetracked by Hill and watching the news.

"Hey Trixie, just calling to see how ya doing?"

"Girl, I've been trying to catch up on my sleep. Sorry I didn't call you. I know you were worried about me but I'm fine."

"Well, that's good to hear. That LaTasha sounded off the hook!"

"Yeah, she's a straight mess. She was all over some guy name Jonah."

My eyes blinked. "What, what did you say?"

This couldn't be Kyle, I thought. Jonah was Kyle's middle name. He enjoyed using the Hebrew name because it was such a great conversation starter to manipulate a room.

"Jonah. When I met him I thought of the Bible story about him being swallowed up by some fish."

I disregarded her comment. "Where was the party?"

"At some townhouse in Fell's Point. Nice layout with expensive art work and—"

"What does this Jonah person look like?" My curiosity was getting the better of me.

"Dark skin brother, very suave, soft spoken, well dressed, wears a pinky ring—"

"Damn." *It was Kyle.*

"What did you say Deidre?"

"Nothing." I thought, *that motherfucker didn't waste any time.*

"Before the night ended, some more girls came through and it was like a sex party up in there. I told them I had to bounce. When I went to tell LaTasha I was leaving, I saw her giving Jonah a blow job."

"Goodness, this chick sounds like she gets around."

"I guess. She and Jonah must go way back because he was calling her honey and she seemed very familiar with the house."

"I see." I was beginning to get angry at the idea that Kyle didn't hesitate to rescue some woman with not much going on. I didn't understand that "save a ho" syndrome and we often fought over him trying to save these women in distress as if he were a gallant knight on a white horse. I couldn't figure out his attraction to these women except he liked drama and the excitement that he got from meddling in their lives. The sad thing was once he got bored he didn't know how to extract himself from the situation.

"Well, I gotta get ready for the club."

"Oh, okay, I better go check on my pasta before the water dries out. I'll catch up with you later."

After adding some more water to the pasta, I sat down on the kitchen stool trying to process what Trixie had told me in our brief conversation. How deep was Kyle involved with LaTasha?

CHAPTER 12

I WALKED INTO TRINKETS & ART Delights at 10 a.m., turned the alarm off and the lights on. I threw my coat and sweater vest on the counter, rolled up my sleeves and got started on the window display. Fifteen minutes into moving some art sculptures to the far left of the store and placing some Mayan vases on a floor base, I realized that I had left my cell phone in the console of my car and ran out to get it.

The cell phone buzzed with a text message. I thought it might have been from Hill, but when I read it I was warned again.

"STOP DIGGING!"

My heart pounded and I ran back into the shop and locked the door behind me.

I pressed my back up against the door and thought how fortunate I was that I survived the attack a few weeks ago. I blew off the first threatening message and now I was faced with a second threat. Hill warned me about getting a new cell phone, but my stubbornness got in the way. I had always gotten my way, especially since I was an only child. But if I have to choose between living in fear or living in freedom, then I choose the latter. With my creativity dampened, I returned the box of glassware that I was going to place in the window to lure casual browsers into the store for the holidays to the counter and called it a day.

I hit the beltway heading home and noticed that a black Ford F-150 had been following me for a few miles. At first I thought nothing of it until I changed lanes and the driver changed lanes too. When I slowed down or sped up so did the driver of the truck following me. I glanced quickly into the rear-view mirror to see who was driving. I could barely make out anything except a silhouette of the person behind the wheel because the truck had tinted windows and it sported a custom front-end mask which made it look angry.

The truck roared toward me, almost hitting my bumper. I steadied my hands and weaved in and out of traffic amidst pissed off drivers honking their horns and giving me the middle finger. The person driving the truck was either bold or stupid. Who would want to risk causing a major accident on a busy highway and have the police on their ass? Drivers watching this craziness would no doubt be on their cell phones calling the police and they would be here in no time. My cell phone rang and I clicked on my Bluetooth.

"What you doing?" Angela asked, chomping on some chips.

"Girl, I'm in the middle of some crazy shit," I said, switching lanes again.

"Deidre, what's going on?"

"Someone's following me. Trying to kill me," I shouted at her.

"Damn, what the hell? You should be calling the police instead of talking to me."

"I'm trying to lose them but they're on my ass. Damn, here they come again, girl, I gotta go." I clicked off my Bluetooth, tugged on my seatbelt, braced myself, stepped on the gas and cut off a driver trying to get to an exit. The driver angrily shouted, "You stupid bitch!" and zoomed off. *I bet she'll definitely call the police.*

My nerves were rattled. I tried to compose myself. Where the hell are the police when you really need them? I swear, now was not the fucking time for donut breaks. "Shit, shit, shit...here they come again," I said loudly to myself.

Adrenaline pumping, I accelerated the car, this time doing 80 in a 65-mile-per-hour zone. My car swerved a little, my hands were sweaty and I was perspiring. I breathed in deeply, gripping the steering wheel to maintain control. I thanked God for that moment of steadiness. I zinged by more angry drivers, honking their horns, but there wasn't much I could do. I looked into the rear-view mirror and the driver of the truck flashed its high beams as he came charging at me. I held my breath and thought he was going to slam into the back of my car. He skillfully came close enough to side-swipe me, but then suddenly took off onto the next exit.

Heart pounding, I slowed my car to blend with the flow of traffic, still amazed that no sirens or flashing lights were nowhere in sight. Angela called me back.

"Girl, what's going on? You all right?" I heard panic in her voice.

I breathed a sigh of relief before answering, "Girl, whoever it was took off at an exit, but I'm sure that won't be the last of them."

"How could you be so calm? Weren't you scared?"

"You have no idea how much I'm shaking in my Vickie's."

Angela changed her tone. "This is not good. You're trying to solve this murder all by yourself and it's getting to be too much. When are you going to tell Hill what's really going on?"

"He knows all I need him to know—"

"But it's getting too dangerous and you KNOW it."

"Whatever." I brushed her off.

"You won't be saying 'whatever' when your ass ends up dead on the side of the road."

There was silence between us. Angela was right. I guess I never stopped to think what I might be up against. This was real life with real life killers and real life threats. But I still had a burning inside me to get them before they got me.

"Yeah, you're right," I said humbly, nodding my head in agreement.

"So," Angela sighed. "You good for getting home?"

"Yeah, wish I could talk to Hill but he's not answering his phone." "Why, what's up with him?"

"He's in New York. Don't ask, long story."

"I won't. But this was frightening and you need to get in touch with him as soon as you can. Well, let me get off the phone now that I know you're safe."

"Thanks for calling me back. I know this wasn't easy being on the phone with me and not knowing what was coming next..."

"You should've been on the phone calling the damn police like I said. But hey, you seem to know what you're doing," Angela snapped at me with an attitude.

"Right. I really should've but I can't deal with all the paperwork, more questions and more people getting in the way. Next thing you know I'd be on the news and who knows what else."

"Hmm, do you then. You can be so damn stubborn. Just call me when you get home."

"Sure will." I paused for a moment and thanked God I came out unscathed. This incident could've ended up getting major news coverage and a lot of people would probably have been happy and pissed off at the same time. I have always been headstrong, chasing answers and looking for justice as long as I can remember. Only this time, Lia's death heightened the stakes and I had to get to the bottom of things. But was it worth losing my life?

Angela could rest easy now that I told her I would clue Hill in on what I have been up to. The funny thing was, I didn't promise it would be soon. When I hung up, I realized that I may be in over my head, but I'd be damned if I'm going down without a fight. My mind began to go into overdrive and I went into my office and pulled out a yellow legal pad and began making notes of all my moves since Lia's murder. There were a few unanswered questions, like who was sending me threatening text messages and how did they know where I'd be today, but the major question was WHY? What didn't they want me to find out?

My phone number had been unlisted for years, but you could buy pretty much anything on the Internet these days. The fact that my every move was seemingly being tracked had me puzzled, I figured that I must have been lo-jacked. Although the following day is Sunday, my mechanic better be ready to check out my car after church. He would be mad, but the Lord wouldn't mind him helping out a dear friend as I had done several times, sending him referrals for business.

I left him this message after the beep: "*Hey, Rev. It's Deidre. I know it's late but I'm gonna stop by tomorrow. Um, I hope you won't mind checking out my car. Love ya and yeah, blessings!"*

Reverend Wright operated a garage attached to his home. He fixed cars during the weekdays and saved souls on Sundays. Since Lia's death, I'd not been to church to hear the Reverend's good word and I missed it. He had charisma and charm that soothed the aching and lost souls that trudged in every Sunday for blessings, forgiveness or guidance.

As I approached the garage, I heard Kirk Franklin's "Looking For You" playing on the radio. The Reverend was wearing his favorite denim overalls, long-sleeved button-down shirt in a poly blend, and boots. He was tinkering with his 1967 Corvette and singing along.

I walked into the garage, clapping my hands, and singing, *"Jesus you are, you are my sunlight after the rain..."*

He looked up and grinned. "Amen to that. That boy sure knows how to get a congregation going, especially them young kids." He wiped off his wrench with a shop rag, got up from his work bench and gave me a bear hug. "So the prodigal child returns."

I snuggled into his embrace and whispered, "Yes, in the flesh."

He released me from the hug, but held me by my shoulders and looked me in the eyes, then said, "You seem troubled."

I thought I hid my fears well, but the Reverend could always see through them. He had been there throughout the years and I relied on him a lot especially when my father decided to abandon my mother and me for a much younger woman and move to California. My mom was distraught, but the Reverend, my father's best friend, was a big help to her and took me camping with his sons and to other fun places.

He was a great father figure and I wished he was married to my mother. But that would have been problematic as he was already married to a woman who was jealous of the time he spent with me and my mother. So, he resigned himself to loving my mother from a distance.

"I'm fine," I reassured him.

"Humph! I don't quite believe you but okay. Now let's take a look at your precious car."

"Please don't ask a lot of questions, but lately I think someone's been following me."

The Reverend raised his eyebrows and looked at me quizzically. I rested my hand on his shoulder and reassured him again that I was fine. I tossed him the car keys which he caught in midair.

"Work your magic. I know it's your holy day but let's see if you can find out whether I have a tracking device on my car."

"All right, baby girl. Don't know how long this will take but have a seat over there." He pointed to the far corner of the garage. "Grab a drink from the mini fridge."

"Don't mind if I do."

Thirty minutes later, the Rev slid from under my car with the device and confirmed my suspicions. He disabled the system, but did not hold back his tongue. "You know what church folks say?" He was now standing in front of me with his arms folded.

"No, what do they say?" I sipped my soda.

"God don't like when folks act ugly. What's really going on with you?"

"I hear that but when folks meet the devil, it's okay to act ugly." Little did he know I was getting ready to polish off my gun and go back to the firing range to do some target practice. At least the lessons I got from him weren't wasted and I'm sure he would be proud. I was growing tired of whoever was trying to run me off the road, attack me and worse still, if they tried to hurt any more of my friends.

The Reverend placed his hand on my head, said a short prayer and then said, "Blessings, my child." He then took off his sterling silver cross necklace and pressed it into the palm of my right hand. "Take this. Safe travels."

My eyes teared up for a moment. "Thanks, Rev. I'll be careful."

I sat in my car and stared at him as he waved goodbye to me. I then looked up and saw the curtains in the upstairs bedroom close and knew that his wife was watching us the entire time. I smiled to myself and eased out of the paved driveway ready to map out my next move.

CHAPTER 13

I PLAYED WITH THE CROSS CHAIN around my neck while I contemplated what to make for dinner. I opened the fridge and shook my head at its bare contents of wine, string cheese, and four eggs. I slammed it shut and decided to run to the grocery store to buy some salmon, vegetables, and a salad. I was grabbing my coat and keys when my cell phone rang. I didn't recognize the number but I answered anyway.

"Hello?"

"Hey, lady. It's Russell. Wassup?"

"Hey, Rus. I'm fine, was just getting ready to run to the store," I said cheerfully. I hadn't heard from him since I last saw him at Lia's funeral.

"You're always on the go. Should've called you before to see how ya doing, but I just moved to Atlanta and been busy settling in."

"I guess I should be asking you the same. How ya doing?"

"I'm doing all right. Did you finally divorce dude?" Russell asked.

Russell never liked Kyle and often hinted that he had seen Kyle out at parties and local events with other women. I brushed it off but deep down I was hurt. Russell always said that I was too good for Kyle and wondered what took me so long to see the light. He would constantly tell me that if a man takes away from the assets of a woman then he's nothing but a liability to her. He had so much wisdom about relationships, no wonder he wrote such beautiful love songs especially for his girl, Lia.

I sighed. "Everything was finalized last week and I'm over it," I lied. I was still hurting, but I'd tried putting a positive spin on it. It was difficult shoving the past seven years into the recess of my mind, but some days I loved to hate Kyle. He had a magnetic quality about him that would make me sometimes forget my own thoughts. He knew which buttons to push and overall was an awesome lover. But I now had to move on and Hill seems a likely candidate. Just seeing how much he loved his wife and how devoted he was to her, made him so attractive to me. One day if I played my cards right, I hope he would show me that same kind of love and devotion. I just had to pray that I would be around to enjoy it.

"Any word on the investigation? I'm sure you'd call if they caught those sons of bitches," Russell said angrily.

"Don't worry. I'm keeping a close eye on it."

"Cool. Well, you got my new number and like I said don't be a stranger. Holla at a brotha if you need some advice about your next man," Russell said laughing.

"I'm not quite ready but I'll let ya know when I need the 411 on how you men roll."

"I'd love to see you let your hair down and not be so uptight but you just need the right kinda brotha to bring the real Deidre out," he said teasingly.

"What you saying, I'm boring and stiff?"

"Can be. You know that's why I call you a square."

"I always wondered why you called me that," I laughed.

"Well, you're not the typical sister. You have rules, everything has to be just right, and you're always on time."

"Damn skippy. I don't have to be on CP-time like the rest of us!"

"True, true. See that's why we get along. I understand a sister like you. Lia was like that too, but she knew how to relax and chill with a brotha like me. You know her peeps didn't approve of us dating but she didn't care. I guess she told them huh, even when I acted like a fool that one time at her family's Christmas party."

"Yeah, I remember. But you were also good for her. You showed her how to laugh, be spontaneous and have fun."

"And I want that for you. Just hope you find it soon," he said.

I heard a click on the phone. "Is that your phone or mine?"

"That's yours girl! Let me let you go. Holla back soon."

"I will," I said, then I clicked over. "Hello? Hello?"

There was no answer, just dead space and heavy breathing. I waited for a second and boldly said, "Bring it," before the phone went dead. This pissed me off and I marched directly to my bedroom closet. I opened the doors, reached toward the back and pulled out my lockbox that was buried behind some boxes. I unfolded the cloth that kept my gun warm and made sure it was within reach in my nightstand drawer, should I get an unwanted guest in the middle of the night.

The car chase rattled me and I wanted to talk to Hill so badly. I called him several times, but the calls went directly to his voicemail. I called the police station and was told that he took some time off and wouldn't be back for a few days. So I was really surprised when I finally got a hold of him early this morning and told him to meet me at the shooting range off I-295 North in Severn.

At 11 a.m. sharp, Hill pulled up and parked next to my car. I opened the passenger side door to let him in. When he sat down, I handed him a cup of coffee that was still piping hot. He took a sip while his eyes penetrated mine.

"What's going on, Deidre? You sounded so abrupt this morning," he said.

"Well, how would you feel if someone tried to run you over!" I exclaimed.

"What? Calm down and tell me what happened."

"Someone driving a black Ford F-150 was following me when I left the antique shop two days ago and tried running me off the road. I was scared as hell but I managed." I was upset because he wasn't around but I had to realize that he had his own demons to deal with.

"I'm sorry I wasn't there for you. But you know I had things to take care of." "Yeah, how did that work out for you?" I asked him.

"It didn't," he said, hanging his head low.

"What do you mean?"

There was a long pause before he answered, as if he were trying to find the right words. "It was just another dead end in the Moonlight Strangler case. It was a copycat. This fool was caught breaking into someone's house around midnight wearing all black with some rope in a bag. He even announced himself as the strangler. How dumb was that?" He laughed. "He didn't anticipate that his victim's boyfriend would be home and that they would tie his ass up and call the police."

"You must be disappointed."

"That's putting it mildly. I really thought the police had caught the bastard but he's still out there," he said heatedly.

I quickly changed the subject. "So, ah, you just hung out for a few days."

"Yeah," he said in an even toned manner. "Caught up with some of the fellas from the precinct and visited my aunt in Flatbush."

"That's good. I see you're still tight with your fellow NYPD officers."

"Yeah, they supported me when I was going through some stuff. Good set of guys. They tried talking me into coming back to the precinct."

"And?"

"And, I didn't give them an answer."

"So you're thinking about it." I thought, *damn am I going to lose him to the big city and bright lights?*

"Dunno. I'm warming up to Maryland." He smiled and reached for my hand.

I smiled too but then brought the conversation back to the investigation. "Did you hear about the drug raid in Baltimore a few days ago?"

"Yeah, yeah, some of the officers were talking about it. That was a major drug bust."

"Hill," I said quietly. "Um, I think I recognized one of the guys they arrested."

"Really? Who?"

"Remember when I came to see you at the station a few weeks ago when you were interviewing the witness?"

"Yes," he said sipping his coffee.

"This same guy, the one with a scar across his neck, was being hauled away in the station that day..." I paused. "Three years ago, he threatened to kill me after I prosecuted him on a drug charge."

"And do you think he's part of Taevon's crew?"

"Could be. When I saw him on the news, he was limping on his left leg. I wounded my attacker on that same leg. Coincidence?

Humph."

"Let me look into it. Do you remember his name?"

"Cuttie Banks. How could I forget." I lowered my eyes.

He pulled a notebook out of his jacket pocket and jotted down the name. "If it's the same guy and he's working with Taevon you could be in serious trouble. But I'm still trying to find the connection. You sure you haven't pissed off anyone?"

"Ah, yeah quite sure." Now I'm thinking *he's pissing me off.* How could he ask me such a question. It's not like I go around picking fights with people. I had my share of enemies when I worked as a prosecutor in the narcotics unit. But I left that world and had now settled into a different life where the only thing that could possibly threaten me would be a bad window display.

"So what's up with meeting at the firing range? I know you're not planning on going all Dirty Harry on me." He leaned back in his seat and pretended to take out an imaginary gun from a side holster, fired it up into the air, blew the smoke from it, and then placed it back into the holster.

Although the pressure of finding Lia's killer and being attacked was getting to me, Hill somehow managed to diffuse it even if it was only for a little while. I liked that about him.

"Just needed to brush up on my skills. A girl can't be too careful these days," I said, smiling.

The indoor firing range was located in a shopping mall. Walking in, we observed a flurry of activities: people were in line waiting to register for a lane, others were looking at firearms, ammunition, gun accessories, and admiring the targets. Hill and I read the range rules and regulations, signed the agreements and left our drivers' licenses with a staff member. We purchased thirty minutes of range time, two boxes of ammunition, ear plugs, eye and ear protection and selected our paper targets. When we walked into the firing area, several men were busy firing at their targets and I watched as the shells kicked back and fell to the floor. We found our lane and Hill told me to go first. I took my gun out of its pouch, laid it on the side pocket of the booth, loaded the ammunition into the clip, inserted the clip into my gun and sent my target toward the back of the room.

Hill looked at me and asked, "Do you know how to use that thing?"

"We'll see." I secured my ear muffs and adjusted my shooter's glasses.

"Hold it...don't jerk," he said, standing behind me and holding my hands steady on the weapon. His closeness made my heart beat a little faster and I could feel the heat rising from his body. I had to focus, but it was getting increasingly hard for me as I inhaled his aftershave.

"I got it, I got it," I said, hoping he would back away from me. I pulled the trigger and hit my target. "Bull's eye, right in the chest." I pumped my fist in the air like Tiger Woods after a victory on the greens.

He pulled up my paper corflute target. "Deidre, who knew? Where'd you learn to shoot like that?" He was impressed. So was I. It had been years since I've fired a weapon. The Rev had taught me well during those summers I spent with him and his sons camping, hunting, shooting cans, and bottles at Patuxent River State Park. Little did I know those skills would come in handy one day.

"A lady should have some secrets." I smiled.

"I see you're a woman of many talents, beautiful yet tough. But I sense something else in you that's not quite settled."

"And you're a man of many talents as well, handsome yet gentle." I saw him blush then smile. There was no denying there was chemistry between us. We vibed and I liked it.

CHAPTER 14

L ATELY, I'VE HAD TO BE creative in bringing in additional revenue to the antique shop by advertising it as a space for performances and exhibitions. Early this morning, I was reviewing a proposal from François, a prima donna artist who wanted to have his art exhibition this upcoming Friday. I didn't have a lot of time and several changes had to be made before I got to the shop.

I shook my head at the request for a scantily clad waiter, a phallic ice sculpture centerpiece, and escargot as an appetizer. I drew a red line through these items and recommended a fully clad waiter, a floral centerpiece and appetizers which included shrimp kabobs, buffalo wings, mini quiches and crab rangoon. I flipped to the second page of the proposal and shook my head again. This time, he wanted me to remove my art pieces so his art work would get all the attention. This request got a red line as well and I made a note to talk to him about changing the dynamics of the shop. I wasn't in the mood for interruptions, but welcomed a call from Trixie.

"Hey, Deidre. Hope I'm not interrupting. Anyway, real quick, gotta tell you what happened this past weekend."

"Mmm-hmm," I said, while reviewing more recommendations.

"I saw Jonah talking to Marvin and it was getting heated. They were arguing, getting all loud."

"What was all the fuss about?"

"LaTasha."

This sounded interesting. I wondered why Kyle would be so interested in LaTasha's employment. I put my pen down and waited to hear more. "What did she do now?"

"She put a beat down on another dancer because she thought the poor girl was checking out Jonah. She kept going on and on about how Jonah was her man while she kicked the girl in the stomach."

"Damn. This chick got some serious anger management problems." I shook my head and thought, *I'm not really surprised*. Women tended to go crazy once they had a taste of Kyle, or Jonah, or whatever he was calling himself these days. He enjoyed conquering these women and riding the high he got from watching them fight over him. However, once the newness was over, he liked watching their reactions when he would no longer return their calls. I remember on one occasion when we were having lunch in Fell's Point, a tall slender brown-skinned woman came over to the table, glared at me and asked him what he was doing having lunch with me. Clearly, she had no idea I was his wife. I stared at her and she stared back at me, indicating she was ready to whoop my ass. I shook my head, then looked at him, threw my napkin on my plate and left them yelling at each other. I guess I should've taken it to the streets and beat her ass, but I wasn't cut out like that. From there, the relationship began going downhill as I watched him get sloppy with his sexcapades.

Trixie's voice came back into focus. "Yeah, she's *scared* of no one and carries a switchblade in her purse. She doesn't back down from a fight and some of the other dancers are afraid of her. She's hood!"

"And you? Aren't you a little scared?"

"Sometimes, but I can hold my own. Plus I got Cassius."

"Yeah, but he can't always be with you."

"I know. But let me finish...Marvin was about to fire her but Jonah stepped in and said he wouldn't allow it."

"What?" *It's so typical of Kyle to control everybody around him*, I thought.

"I guess he and Marvin must be business partners or something because she's still working there."

I had to grit my teeth to fight off my anger. I always wondered why Kyle wouldn't come home early on Friday nights. I get it now;

he was busy seeing LaTasha and she was shaking her ass in his face while he was throwing dollars her way. Although the divorce was over I was curious about the kind of hold LaTasha had on Kyle. For a smart man he lacked common sense. I had protected him for many years, but now he had to watch out for himself.

"Um, Trixie, are you working at the club tonight?"

"Yeah, later on. Why?"

"I have a meeting at the Harbor Court Hotel at the Inner Harbor. Why don't I pick you up and we can grab a late night dinner?"

"That'd be great. I'll ask Marvin if I can dance early so I can get out by nine."

"Okay, I'll see if I can stop in and see you dance. Are women allowed inside?"

"Yes, Marvin doesn't give a damn as long as they pay high prices for those watered down drinks. Mostly, it's just men up in there but sometimes they would come in with their ladies to get their freak on."

"Well all right then."

"I haven't had a nice meal in a while. Shoot, all Cassius needs is some lake trout, couple slices of bread or a chicken box from the corner store and he's good to go."

"Oh, don't forget his half and half," I said with a laugh.

"I know, right? I can't drink lemonade and iced tea mixed together. Ugh, taste bitter to me."

"Looks like things are going well between you two," I said.

"I really like him. He's got potential."

"I think you're good for him."

Trixie chuckled. "I think so too. Oh, snap."

I heard a horn blow. "Is that Cassius?"

"Yup. He's always on time to pick his baby up." She giggled. "I'll tell him we're going out later. Oh, before I forget, Marvin is having a male stripper troupe called Whip Appeal performing at the club tonight. It's gonna be crazy up in there with all those women spending their hard-earned cash.

See you soon."

Did she just say male stripper troupe?

The sounds of Ludacris came thumping through the doors of

the Kitty Kat Club and spilled out onto the pavement when I pulled up. After my Executive Board Meeting at Helping You Up, a mentoring program for teenage girls, I dodged some of the nosy board members and slipped into the ladies room to change into my club gear. Within thirty minutes I walked out of the Harbor Court Hotel transformed into a club diva: wearing a Mary J wig, a black mini-skirt, a tight red ruffled blouse, thigh high boots, leather jacket, high shine lip gloss, and popping gum with an attitude. Thankfully, no one saw me.

The parking lot was crammed, but I finally found a space where I had to pray my car doors didn't get dinged while I was in the club. I got out of the car, slung my bag over my shoulder and walked quickly up to the club but stopped in my tracks when I saw a black BMW Z3 with vanity plates "BOW2ME." *Damn, Kyle's inside.*

I didn't know how I would react if I saw him with LaTasha hugged up in blissful harmony. I shrugged off the feeling and joined the long line that was snaked around the block.

The women in line were very anxious to get in. They wore the shortest and tightest pants or skirts, the tightest tops, weaves down their backs, stiletto heels that could double as weapons, fishnet stockings, and too much perfume. I looked at myself and I looked like them. When the line moved up they would shove the person in front of them a little closer. At first, I thought a few fights would break out but nothing happened. I guess they all wanted to get in to see Whip Appeal and didn't want to risk getting kicked out of line.

A car passed by and a passenger yelled out, "Yo ladies y'all looking good enough to eat tonight. Hmm." A few of the woman hollered back, "You know it!"

This was going to be an interesting night. Before I got to the back of the line, I heard a woman on her cell phone chatting away and rocking from one foot to another. I looked down at her shoes and could tell they were brand new and hurting her feet.

"Yeah, girl, you better hurry up 'cause I can't hold your spot in line for too long. What? Jus' give the nigga some and keep it moving," she said. "Girl, you know how I love me some Whip Appeal, saw them in D.C. last month. Uh-huh."

Yes, I was definitely in for a treat. I had never seen Whip

Appeal perform before, but I guessed they were worth the price of admission. I watched the burly bouncer standing at the door turning folks away. I didn't know whether he had a private list or if they didn't look the part, but I was prepared to work my magic and get into the club. Although it was cold outside, he was wearing a black T-shirt which hugged his massive body and squeezed his bulging, heavily tattooed arms. Looking at the intricate inked design that graced his body almost made me dizzy.

I walked up to him and flashed a very pretty smile while rubbing on his right arm. He smiled and said, "Wassup li'l mama?"

"Ain't nothing," I said, popping gum to calm my nerves. I hadn't been out to the club by myself in a long time, and when I did I was meeting some of my other girlfriends. We had each other's backs, but tonight I had to watch out for myself.

"Looking cute tonight," he said, making a sucking sound with his mouth and giving me a lecherous look.

"Yeah, you like?" I spun around to give him a good view.

He folded his arms and looked down at me. "Cover tonight is twenty bucks."

"Cool, I can afford that." I gave him the twenty dollars and he ran his wand slowly up and down my body. He lingered more than usual until I said, "That should be enough now. I ain't got nuthin' on me."

He gave me a devilish grin. "Just making sure I cover all my bases."

I looked up at him and rolled my eyes. "Riiight."

"Such a tight ass body, hmm," he said, removing the velvet rope and letting me in.

Smoke from cigars and cigarettes filled the inside of the club and irritated my contact lenses, but I blinked twice to adjust my eyes. The music was bumping out of the speakers all over the club; female dancers were giving lap dances while others performed on stage. I wandered through the crowd in search of Trixie and kept an eye out for Kyle. I ordered my favorite drink, Grey Goose with cranberry juice at the bar and gave the bartender a tip. Most of the men sitting at the bar were fixated on the girls on stage. By the looks on their faces, they had probably spent their entire pay checks throwing dollars at the stage. The others who had some money left beckoned for me to keep them company, but I just raised my glass telling them to have a good time.

The music stopped when Marvin stepped on the stage and tapped the microphone. "Mic check one. Mic check two. Hey y'all men should get up outta here. It's officially ladies night." He shaded his eyes from the lights and looked out into the crowd. "Ladies put your hands up for Whip Appeal!"

The crowd erupted in applause. The lights dimmed as the DJ cued up the group's signature song "Whip Appeal" by Baby Face. My eyes were locked on the stage as the curtain pulled back to reveal five well-oiled men from the deepest shade of chocolate to the color of chestnut wearing nipple rings and dressed in red silk drawstring pajama bottoms.

I heard one man grumbling, "Man I don't give a fuck. I paid my money up in 'ere and I'm stayin' till I finish my drink. Where the female dancers at?" He strained his neck to look around.

The Whip Appeal dancers took off their pajama bottoms in sync, twirled them around above their heads and then threw them into the crowd. They were now wearing red slinky G-strings. The women went wild, some were jumping up and down clapping, others were rushing to get a pair of the pajama bottoms, while others threw dollar bills on the stage.

I was enjoying the show but could feel someone watching me. When I turned around, I didn't recognize anyone. I returned to my drink and within a few minutes, I heard a very hearty laugh that could only belong to Kyle coming from the back of the club. I picked up my drink and followed the laughter.

As I got closer, I saw that the area was roped off—VIP section, nothing less for Kyle, the big baller. A woman was sitting on his lap and he was rubbing on her leg. His pinky ring glistened when the light hit it. There was more laughter, she tossed her hair and then rested her head on his shoulder. This pose was all too familiar, a light went on inside my head: the picture that I found in his drawer was taken here with that same woman with a tattoo of a bunny on her leg. The woman turned around, it was LaTasha.

"Hey, Jonah baby. Want me to get you another Absolut

Trouble?" she asked loudly enough for everyone to hear.

"Yeah, baby. Tell the bartender not to skimp on the Grand Marnier," he replied.

LaTasha got up from his lap and kissed him on his lips. He slapped her ass, sank back into his chair and picked up his cigar which was resting in the ashtray. He turned on his cell phone and began typing a text message.

I gulped down the last of my drink and put the glass on the tray of a waitress passing by. I was getting ready to face off with him, but stopped myself wondering why I was so full of anger. I reminded myself that he was free to do whatever and see whomever he wanted and so was I. By the time I decided to make a U-turn and head back to the bar, LaTasha was in my face. She was wearing a tight royal blue spandex dress and a weave past her shoulder. I could smell alcohol on her breath.

"Bitch, why you looking at my man?" she said, giving me a neck twist.

"Look girl, I don't know what you're talking about so you better get outta my face." I shook my head in disbelief as I was now face-to-face with Kyle's lover. I couldn't believe this was the type of woman he would be involved with. To the public, he was a highly respectable and visible businessman. He conducted seminars, donated money to charities, received community awards, but still loved women who brought him drama.

"No, you don't bitch. I saw you," she said, convincing herself. Her words were slurring.

"How? It's dark up in here," I said.

"You was blocking his view."

Oh no. This chick is about to go all Norman Bates on me. She had her purse in her hand and I remembered Trixie saying that she carried a switchblade. I didn't want to hang around to find out if she knew how to use it, but I wasn't backing down if she wanted to start a fight, either. I looked to see if Kyle was on his way over because she was getting louder, but he was gone. I decided she wasn't worth my time or my energy and as I turned to leave, she snatched my hand and spun me around.

"Are you dissing me, bitch?" she asked with much attitude.

I pushed her into a table and held my finger to her face. "You have one more time to call me a bitch and I'll yank that weave out your head." Normally I would be cool, but she pissed me off and since I doubted anyone would recognize me, I was ready to do some damage at the Kitty Kat Club. She reached into her purse. I stepped back, my defenses went up, and I punched her in the face.

When I backed up, I could smell smoke in the air. Someone shouted, "Fire, fire." The fire alarm sounded and suddenly, all hell broke loose. Pandemonium set in as club goers rushed for the exits. Men were throwing women off their laps and stepping over them, bar backs threw down crates of unwashed glasses, the Whip Appeal dancers jumped off the stage, their dicks swinging from side to side, and I got thrown in with the crowd.

Marvin ran to the stage and grabbed the microphone. He shouted, "Yo, Yo. Listen up y'all. Stop pushing. Stop pushing. We're gonna be aight. The fire department gonna be 'ere soon." He threw down the microphone, jumped from the stage and started pushing through the crowd.

A woman with sharp heels stepped on my toes and then pushed me. "Get outta my way bitch," she said as I lost my balance and fell to the floor.

I began coughing as the smoke became thicker. I struggled to get up and that's when I felt someone grab me from behind. I was grateful but as I rose and turned to look at my rescuer, a look of surprise came over my face.

"What the hell...Hill?" I tried scrambling to my feet. He reached around my waist and pulled me up.

"Let's get out of here." He held me tight and plowed through the crowd.

I looked back and saw Kyle pulling LaTasha by the hand. I was thankful that he didn't see me as Hill ushered me through the side doors and to his car. Up ahead, I saw Cassius clutching Trixie's hand as they raced through the front door. I was thankful they made it out. We drove away from all the confusion as I heard the wail of the fire trucks' sirens making their way to the club.

"Deidre, what were you doing back there at the club? Better yet, why are you dressed like this?" Hill asked, quickly looking me up and down.

I wondered the same of him. *Why was he there?* A few moments of silence passed before words came to my lips, "I... can...explain...this."

He reached across my lap, opened the glove box and gave me a tissue. "Here, take this. Wipe your face."

I pulled down the visor which had an illuminated mirror and saw my face full of sweat and dirt. My Mary J wig was off center and my lip gloss was smudged. I pulled the wig off, stuffed it in my bag and cleaned up my face.

Hill looked over at me. "Tell me later."

CHAPTER 15

I WAS MET WITH UNCOMFORTABLE SILENCE: no music, no radio, and no conversation. I eased the seat back, tugged my jacket tighter and closed my eyes not knowing where we were heading or when he would start interrogating me. I didn't care. I almost got trampled on and burned to death in a strip club. I wondered how the *Baltimore Sun* would have reported this incident, *"Former prosecutor dressed like a hooker found dead in a strip club. Was she living a secret life?"*

This had been a close call and I was terrified, but Hill was luckily there to rescue me. About twenty minutes later, he was slowing down. I opened my eyes, yawned, and stretched out my arms as he pulled up into the parking lot of a high rise condominium community. I looked around and realized we were in Canton near the waterfront. I perked up.

Finally, he broke the silence. "Hope you don't mind that I brought you here tonight. Things are getting kinda hot and I need to keep an eye on you."

I smiled. *I didn't mind at all,* I thought. "No, I don't. What about my car?"

"It'll be fine. We can get it tomorrow and then do lunch. How does that sound? You get to choose the place."

"Okay, good."

He parked and we headed toward the building. While we waited for the elevator, I admired the lobby area: marble columns, recessed lighting, flat screen TVs, and black leather chairs against the back wall. The elevator hissed open and Hill hit the button to the fifth floor. When I walked in, he gave me a tour of his well-decorated condo: warm earth-tone colors, gourmet kitchen with granite countertops, stainless steel appliances, cherry cabinets, a sunken bath tub, a master bedroom with floor-to-ceiling windows, and a glass front balcony overlooking the marina and the city's skyline.

"Love your place," I said, pointing to an African mask hanging on one of the walls. "Interesting piece."

"Thanks. Got it when Sierra and I took a trip to Zambia. I like collecting interesting pieces from places that I visit." He picked up a miniature demon wood carving sitting on the fireplace mantle and showed it to me. "Picked this up in Mexico."

I examined it. "Nice. World traveler, huh?"

"When I can get the time, I like to explore new places. Do you like to travel?"

"Yes, been to several places but my favorite are the islands in the Caribbean."

"I see." He put the wood carving back and then turned to me. "You need to get out of those clothes. Let me run you a bath. You can leave your clothes by the door. I promise not to peek at you."

Always the gentleman, I thought. "I'm not worried about that," I said playfully. "Will you join me?"

"Such a tease. I'll let you soak in the tub and I'll jump in the shower in the guest room. Meet me in the living room when you're done." He kissed me on the forehead.

I didn't want to get out of the tub, but the water was getting cold. I stepped out and put on a plush white robe that was hanging on the back of the door. I tied a knot around my waist and walked into the living room. I was greeted by scented pillar candles lit all around the room. I settled into the brown leather sofa and admired the mosaic area rug and more artistry that hung on the walls. He brought me a glass of wine and sat his glass on the coffee table.

He turned on the CD player with a remote and the sounds of Sade, "By Your Side" (The Neptunes Remix) came through speakers in the ceiling. *Damn* he was smooth. I sipped my wine and enjoyed the whole atmosphere. I hadn't been able to relax for a while and it felt good. I smiled inwardly as he lifted my feet, swung them around and laid them on his lap as he sat next to me. I laid back and watched him massage my feet. He was releasing the tension in them, and like a servant aiming to please his master, he began placing gentle kisses around my ankles.

"Hmm." I held the glass off to the side as his kisses crept up my legs followed slowly by his hands. I managed to put my glass on a side table before I spilled every drop of the wine and damaged the carpet. I resumed my position, this time more relaxed and with my legs spread open.

More kisses came and soft moans escaped my lips. I closed my eyes and savored every moment of his caressing. *How did he know that the insides of my legs were my sensitive spot?* I reached out to pull him up for a kiss. He looked at me with hunger in his eyes. My body trembled, ready to betray to me. I felt the river between my legs about to break down my sugar walls and I needed to gain control. He gave me the most delicious kiss, tongue and all. "The Sweetest Taboo" came on and I panicked. "Let's dance."

"What? Now?" He was irritated, but then his demeanor softened.

I said breathlessly, "Yes." His dick was hard and ready to be inside me and now I've thrown him off his game. *Was it too soon? Would I feel guilty?*

He got up and lifted me to my feet. I placed my arms around his neck and he drew me tightly to him. I felt his dick throbbing against me as we grinded until the end of the song. The walls were quickly coming down. *I couldn't resist any longer.* He kissed my neck and then sucked on my lower lip. I threw my head back and moaned even louder. An inner voice commanded, *You need to do this, girl. Release some of the bottled up stress.* I removed his arms from my waist and pushed him down on the rug. I held his arms outstretched above his head as I straddled him.

"Okay, okay, do your thing baby. I don't mind a woman who knows what she wants." He smiled and puckered his lips. "Kiss me."

I slowly and sweetly kissed him and he moaned. I was getting turned on. I took off his T-shirt and ran my fingers through his curly chest hairs.

"Is it my turn yet?" he asked.

My eyes responded yes. He opened the robe and exposed my C cups. He held the softness of my breasts in his hands. "Hmm, nice. Just as I imagined. May I play with the twins?"

"Please," I said softly.

He sat up and held them. He tasted one, teased the other and then switched. *He sure knows how to please,* I thought. *Just do me baby!* He had enough of my teasing and now took control by flipping me over so that he was on top. *Double Damn.* I was breathing heavily, waiting for his next move. He stood up and stepped out of his sweatpants revealing thick muscled legs. He was standing at attention and I knew I was in for a long, slow ride.

"Do you want me?" he asked, kneeling down and spreading my legs.

"Yes," I said in a sensual tone right before he buried his head and tasted my nectar. Unlike Kyle, Hill didn't mind going downtown. He was a master of his game and he hadn't even penetrated me. He continued to lick my clitoris up and down until it started to throb. He curled his tongue and delved deeper into its wetness which made me quiver. He must have sensed that I was ready to buckle because he grabbed his sweatpants, reached into the back pocket and pulled out a condom. He rolled it down his shaft and moved in for the kill. His hugeness filled me up as he entered me with short strokes then longer ones. He kept teasing me and now his thrusts were getting deeper and deeper. I started writhing and moving in tandem with his strokes. The stirring inside me was about to erupt, I grabbed his ass and then dug my nails into his back almost drawing blood.

He kept thrusting and thrusting. "Hold on baby, take me with you," he whispered in my ear. "Just hold...Mmmm...just hold... on...Shit!" I felt him quiver, grunt, his eyes rolled back into his head, and then he collapsed on top of me. He kissed me before pulling out and rolling off to the side. Propping himself up on one elbow, he stared at me and then said, "That's some good pussy!"

"Hmm and that was some DAMN good dick!"

Triple Damn. With our bodies glistening in sweat and my hair all over the place, I asked, "Got one more round in you?" I was greedy. By this time, Sade's "Is It A Crime" came on and I answered affirmatively: *Yes Lawd, it was a crime for me to devour this man.*

☙

We made it to the bedroom, drained and sweaty after round two. My body was totally relaxed and I felt completely safe lying in his arms. At the break of dawn, I woke up and he was missing from my side. I climbed into a pair of his shorts and a sweatshirt he had left for me at the foot of the bed. I walked out into the sunroom and found him wearing only sweatpants and looking through a telescope. I wrapped my arms around his waist and rested my head on his back. "Who knew you could put it down like that? Hmm, you're such a bedroom gangsta."

He laughed. "I guess...ah, thanks. I'm glad I pleased you. Your sex game is tight too."

I slapped him on his ass. "Anything interesting out there?"

Unwrapping my hands from around his waist, he guided me in front of him and gave me the telescope. "See for yourself."

I looked through the lenses and saw the morning fog roll in over the water. The boats swayed lazily back and forth in the marina. "Beautiful."

"Look Deidre, last night was great." He turned me around and held my chin up to his face. "Just so you know, I'm not a one-night-stand kinda guy and would like to start seeing you."

"Like dating," I teased, poking him in his chest.

"Yeah, I may be a little rusty but—"

"You're doing just fine." *I was the rusty one, hesitating to sleep with this man and acting like a shy school girl*, I thought. But that was me, the woman who analyzed everything, the woman who made mountains out of mole hills, and the woman who hesitated to live in the moment, until now.

"Now that we got that out the way, what were you doing at the club last night?"

Moment of truth. I thought he would let the interrogation go, but he was back to business.

I told him all about Trixie, Kyle and LaTasha. He listened without interrupting me and then finally he said, "Do you want to give Daredevil a run for his money?" Before I could answer, he fired at me, "What were you thinking? Let me do my job. That's why I'm on this case."

I guess he told me. I fired back, "I didn't trust that the police would do their jobs—"

"Well, I don't work like that. Every case is important to me. I give it my all and never rest until I get answers. Right now, my hunches are telling me that LaTasha is holding something back. That's why I was there last night to see what she was up to. And now you're telling me that she and your ex-husband are tight." His brows furrowed. "When was the last time you spoke to him?"

"At the divorce," I answered.

"Do you think he could be involved?"

"Wouldn't make any sense. Remember he was shot too. What motive would he have? Lia was a friend. Why would he want her dead?"

"I've seen a lot of things working homicide. It wouldn't surprise me that he would arrange to get shot to cover up his tracks. That's my theory, by the way."

"I doubt it. I still don't know why he would be involved."

"You sure about that?" he quizzed.

"Um, yeah." *Could Kyle be involved?* My heart sank.

"If I find out that he's involved in any way he's going down. You do understand that?"

"Hey, I'm not asking for any special treatment. I just want the truth about who pulled the trigger."

"Justice will be served. Whoever is behind this is jerking us around. Some criminals are smart, but there is no such thing as a perfect crime. Eventually, they will slip up and they'll get caught."

"With you on the clock, I'm sure they'll see the criminal justice system from the other side of the wall," I commented.

Hill paused for a moment before stroking my hand. He looked at me with a longing that I had only seen in Kyle's eyes when he was starting to get serious about our relationship. I gazed back at him knowing that this was the beginning of good things to come despite the cloud that hung over our heads.

CHAPTER 16

WHEN HILL PULLED UP INTO the Kitty Kat Club's parking lot early afternoon, the damage to the club appeared to be minimal except for charring on the outside walls. He kept the engine running. I was reaching for the passenger-side door handle to get out of the car when he said, "Deidre, wait. You forgot something."

"What?" I asked, turning around to face him.

"This." He leaned in for a kiss. "I'm heading to the station. Thought I could spend the day with you today, but I need to get my head back into the case." His voice softened, "Rain check for lunch?"

"Sure. Call me if you get any new information."

He watched me get into my car. I waved goodbye as he drove away. I was glad that he canceled lunch because I had spotted Kyle's car off to the side of the parking lot when we pulled in and wanted to find out why he was still at the club. I drove around the corner and hid my car in a side alley. I moved slowly alongside the wall of the club. When I got close enough, I heard two male voices arguing inside and I peeked into the window of Marvin's office to get a better look.

I saw Kyle and Marvin. They looked like two raging bulls about to come crashing into each other when someone rang the bell at the front door. Kyle stormed out of the office to answer the door while Marvin sat down at his computer. I ducked down before he saw me. He got on the phone and called someone. Shouting at the top of his lungs he said, "If that muthafucka Jonah thinks he can get away with using my money to do whatever he wants, he got another thing coming to him. Him and dat bitch LaTasha think they can play people."

I looked up again and this time I accidentally stepped on a can making a crushing sound. Marvin stopped talking on the phone. *I'd better think fast. I didn't have enough time to run back to the car.*

Marvin flung the side door open. "Who's out 'ere?"

Too late. I was busted. I straightened up, tried not to panic and donned a smile. "Hey Marvin. How ya doing?" I watched his face relax.

"Oh, hey, Private Dancer. Whatchu doin' out 'ere girl? Come in 'ere before you freeze dat ass off."

"Nah, it's all good. Was just wondering if you got any work for a sister. Tryin' to make ends meet you know."

"Outta luck, baby girl. But that chick Trixie you sent me, she sure can dance. She's on point, raking in da big bucks."

"You can't help a sister out? Not even waiting tables?"

"Sorry, boo." Marvin looked at his watch.

I nodded toward the charred walls of the club. "What happened?" I asked, pretending that I wasn't caught up in the commotion last night.

Marvin's eyes followed my nod. "Yeah, dat. Some clown started a fire in the lounge area last night but the sprinkler system got it in time before it caused major damage. Man, the fire department surprised a brotha coming so quick to the spot. You know how it is in the hood. Po-po and everybody else think we don't count."

"I hear ya. When you opening again?"

"Got some cleaning up to do, nuthin' major. We'll be up and jumping soon. Gotta make dat bread. It's rough out 'ere so can't close for too long. Plus the Whip Appeal dancers need to perform again for da ladies. I gave those suckers half on a contract to perform last night."

"Yeah, can't have a bunch of angry women around you." I smiled inwardly, wishing I could come back to see those well-oiled men perform. "Still can't think of anything for a sister to do to make some cash?"

He thought for a moment. "Maybe my boy Jonah could help

you out. He throws a couple of sex parties at secret locations, you know by invitation only." He winked at me.

Didn't know Kyle was such a sex freak. It was amazing how much I was learning about the man I was married to now that we were divorced. It's as if he were living a double life and I was clueless all along. Being with me must have been boring.

"Wanna meet him. He's in da club right now. I'm sure he'd like a pretty one like you. Let me get him," he said, turning to walk back into the club.

I couldn't risk Kyle seeing me. "That's all right. I'll pass on that. Sounds like he's running an escort service to me. I'm not into all that stuff." As curious as I was about what kind of crazy shit he was into, I couldn't risk getting jammed up in a potential bust if he was really operating an escort service.

"Cool. You'll be aight, just find yourself a sugar daddy. He'll pay for dat ass." Marvin's eyes danced all over my body.

"Thanks, Marvin. I'll check in with ya 'cause you never know, right?"

"True. Well aight, gotta get back to da club. Got some business to handle."

As I turned to walk away, I heard Kyle shout out for Marvin to get back to the club because a package came in. I hurried to my car, started the engine and breathed a sigh of relief that he didn't see me. I wondered what Hill would've said to me this time.

After the night that I had and my morning encounter with Marvin, I wanted to sit in front of the TV and do nothing for the rest of the day. But I had to check in with Tori to make sure she was getting things ready for the art show on Friday. I made some popcorn and was about to watch *Judge Mathis* when my cell phone rang. It was Hill.

"Hey." A smile came across my face as I quickly reminisced about the night of passion we'd just had.

"You busy?"

"No. Was about to watch some TV. What's up?"

He cleared his throat. "Got with the officers who made that drug bust a few days ago. Turns out that Cuttie Banks was second in command of Taevon's crew."

"It figures someone just as ruthless as Taevon would be in charge to lead the other foot soldiers. What else did you find out?"

"Well, Cuttie was stabbed to death by another inmate in jail earlier this morning."

"What?" I was stunned.

"From what I hear, he had a lot of enemies. It was probably some unsettled beef. Anyway, I verified that the wound on his left leg was fresh. Like he got it recently. Guess you're right about him attacking you."

"I'm still worried though." *One down, an army to go,* I thought.

"I know. Just hear me out. I was thinking maybe you could spend the nights with me just so I can keep my eyes on you."

I was speechless. *He moved fast.* The invitation was quite tempting. "Thanks, but I...uh, will be all right."

"What if I came to you?" he asked. There was silence between us. "Look Deidre, all I'm trying to do is to make sure you're safe. You can be so stubborn at times."

"You know me. I appreciate the offer, but I'll be fine. There are extra patrols around the neighborhood plus I have ..." I stopped in mid-sentence because I didn't want him to know that I had my gun by my side keeping me safe when he wasn't.

"You win, but if you change your mind," he paused. "You know how to reach me."

"I do."

"Well, I gotta run. The Lieutenant's calling me. Can't believe how much paperwork I have piled up after being out a few days. Be good."

"Hill?"

"Hmm."

"I know I've said it before but thanks for giving this case the focus it deserves."

"Not a problem. I'm here to protect and serve. That's what I do."

"Right. Hey, before you go . . "

"Yes."

"Um, there's an art show at my shop this Friday and I'd like you to be my guest. Hope you can make it if you're not working late."

"Oh, our very first official date."

"Something like that. Pick me up around seven."

"Sure thing, I'll be there."

When the call ended, I sat and pondered Hill's invitation. He was right, I was being very stubborn. He had offered to keep me safe, but my stubbornness wouldn't allow me to let him in. I turned on the TV in time to catch the news reporter mention that Cuttie Banks was killed in jail earlier during the day. I shook my head and thought to myself, *you live by the sword, you die by the sword.* That was just life on the streets. I had hoped Hill would have had a chance to find out from Cuttie who ordered the hit on Lia, but a dead man tells no tale.

I sat at my computer reading e-mails from Tori regarding the recommendations I had made in response to the prima donna's requests.

Tori wrote: *"He's not happy about the appetizers and the centerpiece. He's okay with the store arrangement."*

I replied: *"Sorry this is the East Coast not California. He's such a diva, he'll be fine. Besides where else could he go to get a better deal?"* I hit the send button.

I got up from the computer and headed to the kitchen to go through my mail from yesterday. Just as I was about to open the utility bill, Angela called. "Girl, where you been hiding?"

"Been working. Just signed an artist to use the shop for an exhibition and he's a pain in the ass. Some of his requests are outrageous."

"But he's paying you, right?"

"I know it's all about the benjamins, but should you sacrifice common sense and good taste?"

"Sometimes you got to give people what they want, especially if they paying you."

"I agree, but I do have a say since it's my shop and he's paying me for my recommendations."

"Oh, well that's different," Angela said.

"What's up with you?"

"I'm here brainstorming too. Business kinda slow at the spa. Girl, mothers are cutting back on the extras for their little princesses. So I'm tryin' to find a new angle, maybe have a contest or refer a friend discount."

"That sounds like a great idea. Tough times call for creativity."

"Yeah, so when is this exhibition or whatever you want to call it? Hope it's not by invitation only. I know how you can get all exclusive at times."

"Whatever, I'm sure you'll be there. Um, I invited Hill too," I said giggling.

"What's that I hear? Uh-oh, girl, don't tell me you got some."

"I'm not saying if I did or didn't. Besides, I thought you didn't want to know my business."

"You grown." Angela sucked her teeth.

I could sense that she was pouting. "Okay, if you must know," I paused for emphasis. "I gave him a taste of the goodies last night," I shrieked, stomping my feet.

"And you didn't call me. You so damn secretive, Bruce Wayne ain't got nothing on you," Angela said.

I loved Angela's sense of humor. "Come on girl, you know I don't usually kiss and tell, but brother put it down, girl. Made me want to slap somebody."

"No, he didn't. Can't wait to get all up in his kool aid. He better treat you right."

"Now there you go."

"Well, how you gonna know somebody if you don't ask questions?" she asked.

"True," I said in agreement.

"You really need to ask questions," she reiterated.

Angela was ready to hit me with one of her lectures about asking questions. As for me, I always let things play out, watched people's actions and reactions and sprinkled in some questions, if I were interested. She bypassed all of that and just went straight to the source. She didn't care if some of the questions made you feel uneasy or had you fumbling for the right thing to say. She just had to know. On Friday she would get a chance to question Hill and then let me know whether I should trust him or toss him to the side. Although she met Kyle several years after we got married, her spidey senses kicked in and she warned me that he was up to no good. Behind the charm and the smile, she warned me that Kyle would end up hurting me. I was too blinded by his bullshit and should've listened.

Luckily, my cell phone beeped and spared me the lecture. "Got another call coming in. See you Friday and please go easy on Hill. Don't want you to scare the man off."

"I'll just ask him the basics."

"Thank you!" I clicked over to Trixie's call.

"Deidre, what happened last night? Did you come to the club?"

"Yes, I was there but didn't see you until the fire broke out and Cassius was pulling you out the front door."

"It was crazy in there. I'm glad you made it out too."

"It was close. You really want to go back there?" I asked.

"Don't know. But I've been thinking that I've had enough of dancing at the club. I'm getting tired of the men pawing at me and Cassius getting pissed off all the time. I keep telling him that I don't do lap dances but he keeps showing up like he doesn't trust me. It's not even worth the arguments. I don't want him to get hemmed up and go to jail if he gets into a fight. Plus it looks like LaTasha is going to be in charge of all the dancers."

"Really?"

"I can't stand her. I'm gonna call Marvin and tell him I'm done working for him. I hope you can get whatever other information you can without me. I did my best."

"Don't worry Trixie. I got enough. Thanks, for being such a trooper."

"Cassius will be so happy when I tell him that I'm quitting the club."

"I wish you both the best. He's a good one, can be a little rough around

the edges at times, but he has a good heart."

"Not to mention handy too. If you ever need anything fixed around your house just give him a call. I'm glad he stopped running the streets since he got the job at the Express Jiffy Lube. He wants to go back to automotive school," Trixie said proudly.

"That's a good thing. What about you?"

"I still have my job at Frederick's so I guess I'll ask for some overtime if they have it."

"Yeah, jobs are tight right now. I guess I'll start hitting you up for some store discounts when I drop by."

Trixie laughed. "Anytime girl."

CHAPTER 17

SOMETHING SNAPPED OUTSIDE MY BEDROOM window. I looked at the clock, it was 1 a.m. Instinctively, I reached for my gun from the nightstand drawer. I rolled off the bed and got low to the ground. My heart was beating fast. What if I have to use this weapon today? I've never killed anyone before. I had to remain calm and alert. The sound became louder like the sound of the wind kicking up several tin cans. I was ready to face whatever it was when suddenly, I looked through the window and saw a raccoon jumping out of the trash can. Scared the hell out of me. I exhaled and put my gun back in the drawer for safekeeping.

Since Lia's death I had become very jumpy. Every sound unnerved me. It wasn't easy being here alone these days not knowing whether I would get another threatening text message or someone would try to kill me. Lately, it became a ritual to double check all the windows and doors before I went to bed and make sure I saw the light from the alarm system indicating the system was set.

I felt unsettled in my own house and not knowing how all the pieces fit, puzzled me and kept me up most nights. I was usually good at putting things together quickly, but my patience was getting the better of me. The red tape of following all the rules on this case was getting old real fast and I needed answers. Sleep wasn't a friend of mine and I knew Kyle suffered from insomnia and would be up all night. This case was about to get a nudge.

I picked up the phone and dialed Kyle's number. "We need to talk," I said when he picked up the phone.

"Hey baby, miss daddy?" he asked softly.

I heard a door close. "I know about you and LaTasha." I didn't have time for pleasantries not at this time of night and especially not when I was pissed that he chose to be with a stripper.

"Huh?" He sounded dumbfounded.

"Don't act dumb with me. You heard me. I said...I...know... about...you...and..."

"Damn. How'd you find out?"

"How long, Kyle or is it Jonah? How long has this relation-ship been going on?"

"A few years."

"What? A few years? Right under my nose. Why? What didn't I give you? You know what? Don't even answer that." It was as if a dagger had penetrated my heart. "You can take the girl from the streets, but you can't take the streets out of the girl. So tell me Kyle, were you able to find your fair lady?"

"Shut your fucking mouth," he said in an indignant tone.

"I'm not scared of you. You son of a bitch," I retorted. I wasn't surprised at his response. Whenever I called him out on something, he would get really mad and try shutting me up.

"What the fuck do you want from me? We're divorced now so you shouldn't give a damn about what I do or who I'm fucking."

"I do when the bitch may have killed Lia and shot your dumb ass!" I snarled at him.

A few seconds passed before he answered, "I don't believe you. Why are you in the middle of this? Let the police do their jobs. What proof do you have anyway?"

"Wouldn't you love to know," I said taunting him. "You better watch your back and think with the right head. Danger may be closer than you think, or is it lying in your bed?"

He shouted, "You bitch." Then I heard a click in my ear. I smiled. The seed was planted. I had ruffled a few feathers and now sleep was a friend of mine, but not for too long.

I was staked out across the street from Kyle's townhouse. I pulled the baseball cap close on my head and slid down into the seat as I watched LaTasha come out the front door. I looked at the clock on the dashboard, it was 6 a.m. She was casually dressed in tight jeans, a short fur coat, and her hair was pulled back in a ponytail. She stood on the steps, lit up a cigarette, and blew it into the morning air. She looked up and down the street before getting into her car which was parked in front of the house. I shook my head. I never smoked and Kyle always said that he would never kiss a woman who smoked. He lied.

I stayed two car lengths behind her and made a mental note of her license plate. She stopped at a red light and flicked the cigarette butt out the window. I followed her to East Baltimore where she parked in front of a row house. I drove by casually but looked in the rear-view mirror to see where she entered. I stopped two blocks away and wrote down the license plate number and the street address before it escaped my mind. I was heading to my side of town when I decided it was time to call in my cavalry. I dialed Marcusetta's phone number.

"Wake up, I know you're not sleeping."

"Why you always *cawling* me when I'm tryin' to get my sleep on?"

"I know you. You're probably just getting in from the streets."

"Yup. Went out drinking with some of my homegirls."

"Look, I got something I want you to ask Cassius to check out. He's not answering his phone."

"Tsk. I shouldn't have answered mine, either," Marcusetta said.

"What did you say?"

"Just kidding. Whatchu need that you gotta mess with my sleep?" "You need to write it down."

"Hol' up. Let me get something to write with." I heard Marcusetta fumbling around. "I'm back. Go ahead."

I gave her the address and told her to have Cassius check it out and report back to me.

"Hey, Deidre. This part of town is no joke. That's where most of the stash houses are."

"And that's why I want Cassius to check it out. He can handle himself and he probably grew up with some of these guys."

"I don't know if they'll trust him. He's been off the streets for a while and is happy now that he hooked up with Trixie. Met her the other day. Cool sistah."

"I know I'm asking a lot, but I'm calling in my favors," I said.

"I feel you. Don't worry. He'll do you this solid."

An image of Cassius flashed across my mind. He was seventeen when he was arrested with some other guys being recruited by a local gang. The look I saw on his face told me that he was lost and looking to belong somewhere. I made a deal with his attorney that gave him probation. When the case was over I pulled him to the side and told him that he could achieve anything he wanted if he stopped following others and be his own leader. He gave me a hug and thanked me for believing in him. He also said that if ever I needed anything, he owed me one. I'm sure he wouldn't think that this favor would put him in the den of lions.

"Marcusetta, please tell Cassius to be careful."

"Yeah, I'll let him know. He's like family and for your sake he better not get hurt."

"Look, he can always say no. Have him call me if he doesn't want to do this for me." I was more than aware of the burden of this favor. If anything were to go wrong I would have Trixie to answer to as well.

"Aight," Marcusetta said before ending the call.

I drove home in silence and mulled over the day's events. How far was I willing to go to find answers? Hill reassured me that he was on the case. But the high that I got from running around trying to find answers could not be duplicated working in my antique shop and deciding which art pieces to put on sale.

I realized that I had people I cared about and I couldn't risk losing them. I gave them a choice so it was up to them whether they were willing to take on the challenge. I knew Cassius could handle himself. He was far from being stupid and he had street smarts. While some of the guys would brag about driving fancy cars and rolling in cash, they still respected that Cassius was happy holding down a nine-to-five job. There were times when he would miss being on the streets, but I would remind him that he was still six feet above ground while many of his friends were either locked up, strung out, hiding from the law, or dead. He would think about it and then put on his uniform with his name tag sewn in the upper left hand corner, pack his lunch, and head to work.

Ten minutes later my cell phone rang. It was Cassius. "Hey Deidre." "Hey back to ya. I see you got my

message. Well?"

"It's all good. I owe you and now you're cashing in. I can dig it."

"Thanks, Cassius. This means a lot to me."

"I know," he said.

"I wouldn't ask if it weren't important."

"Marcusetta told me about your friend."

"I know this is a rough crowd and you may know some of them, but be careful. Get the hell out of there if something doesn't look right. I don't want to have to—"

"Yeah, you'd have a lot of explaining to do," he said, cutting me off.

"Let me let you go. Call me as soon as you know something," I said.

"Bet."

I wished that I could blink and have these past few weeks disappear. I wished that Lia were still here. I missed my friend and the closeness we shared and the things we had planned to do that we would never do. I hated feeling helpless. My marriage was over but sometimes I was angry that Kyle didn't fight hard enough to save it. He had no remorse for his behavior and I hated that he was so cocky to think I would put up with it forever. This was a lot to deal with and I hadn't had a chance to process everything. Hill was a great guy, but I didn't want to rush into anything too fast. So far he had been nothing short of charming. He was very protective and could deal with me being headstrong and stubborn at times.

I needed some words of wisdom and guidance because I was becoming unraveled. I called the person I trusted the most to give me what I needed. He answered on the first ring. "Hey, Deidre."

"Hi Rev, hope I'm not intruding."

"Oh no, you know I always have time for you."

A broad smile came across my face. I recalled when I was in high school and my mother couldn't make it to one of my debate team competitions because she had to work late. I was disappointed, but got my confidence back when I looked out into the audience and saw Reverend Wright waving frantically at me before he sat down. My team made the best argument and we won the competition. At the end of the competition, I ran out into the audience to greet him. He gave me flowers and then told me that my mother had called him and although he was fixing an engine in a vintage car, he took the time to be there for me. I was grateful.

I remained silent for a minute.

"What's on your mind? No need to be shy around me," he said.

"It's this investigation. I'm getting anxious and want it to be over, but I know I have to be patient. Some days I'm fine, but I want things to be back to normal. I just want to stop looking over my shoulder and stop worrying if someone is trying to kill me—"

"Kill you? What's been going on? How deep are you into this? Last time I checked you left the world of crime-fighting to operate an antique shop in Georgetown."

I sighed. "I did, but I was so upset about Lia's death that I jumped right in like a caped crusader trying to solve the case myself. Since then I've received threatening text messages, crank calls, and someone chased me on the highway."

"Deidre, you've always been cautious but this case is making you go through some changes. It's getting too dangerous and I don't want to be the one praying over you any time soon. So let the police do their job."

"Yeah, yeah, yeah. That's what everybody keeps telling me even the police." *The Reverend had a point, but I wasn't ready to admit it.*

"Well there you go, so why don't you listen for a change?"

"I know I should, but I'm so close to getting some new information which the police haven't been able to get yet."

"And how much trouble are you likely to get into for it?"

"If I play the cards right, not much. It's just snooping around, asking some questions."

"Ah," he let out a deep sigh.

I recognized this sigh. It's the sigh that came before one of his sermons. After all, I did call for some wisdom and guidance. "Drop your knowledge, Rev."

He laughed. "I see you know where I was headed. Sorry, no

sermons or lectures from me this evening. But I want you to come to church this Sunday. No excuses. I want to see you there."

I had no choice but to agree. "Okay."

"I didn't get a chance to talk to you about Kyle. But how are you doing?"

"Coping. Some days I try not to dwell on the pain," my voice cracked. I regained my composure. "I try not to blame myself for letting things go on for so long. But I've met someone—"

"Well, who's the lucky fella and when do I get to meet him?"

"He's the detective assigned to the case."

"I see. How's he handling the fact that you're pig headed and tend to like things your way?"

"Always the jokester, huh. He's right on time for me."

"Well, have him tag along on Sunday. Can't wait to meet him."

"We'll see," I said.

"Um, if you don't have anything to do after the service, I want you to come over for dinner. I'm almost positive you have nothing to eat in your refrigerator. Besides, you need some nourishment."

"Right again. Let's just take baby steps. I'll be in church, but I can't promise that I'll come over for dinner. For some reason, your wife never liked me and I'm not in the mood to deal with her."

"Pshaw. Don't mind her. I'm in charge of that house. You can't help that you're the spitting image of your mother. She knows how much I cared for your mother. Why don't you sleep on it and then let me know?"

Sitting at the dinner table with Mrs. Ethel Wright wasn't something I was looking forward to. But I would consider it for the Reverend's sake if Hill tagged along to act as a buffer. Thinking back, Mrs. Wright always turned her nose up at me whenever I came around even though the Reverend treated me like family. He would extend the invitations for her to join us at picnics, movies, and the circus, but she always found an excuse not to come along. I didn't pay it any mind when I was younger, but now it was getting on my nerves.

I thought long and hard before I answered, "We'll see."

CHAPTER 18

FRIDAY NIGHT WAS FINALLY HERE. I was nervous about making my debut with Hill in public and introducing him to my friends. I slipped into the cutest bra and panty set I had in preparation for a private after party with Hill, this time at my house. I sprayed my favorite perfume, *Light Blue* by Dolce & Gabbana in the air and walked into the mist. The doorbell rang as I was zipping up my little black dress. Hill was fifteen minutes early and when I opened the door he surprised me with a bouquet of flowers and planted a kiss on my cheek.

"Thanks." I took the bouquet and rested it against my chest. "For little old me?"

"Woman, you're funny."

I took the bouquet and headed to the kitchen to put it in a vase. I glanced over my shoulder, and saw him looking in the mirror, picking lint off his jacket.

"These are so beautiful." I took a whiff of the bouquet before placing it on the coffee table.

"Almost as beautiful as you are," he smiled as his eyes seductively roamed my body. "Loving that dress you're wearing. Almost ready?"

"Yeah, I'm just getting my coat," I said, reaching into the closet and pulling it off the hanger.

"Here, let me help you with that." He took my coat and slipped it on me. "There you go." He then kissed me softly on my neck.

"Aren't you the perfect gentleman?"

"My momma taught us boys well."

"Oh, so you have a brother?"

"Yes, I haven't had much of a chance to talk about my family or find out about yours since we've been trying to solve this case."

"I know. So where's he?" I picked up my clutch purse and my house keys from the jeweled trinket box on the glass-topped table next to the door. I waited for an answer, but none came. I looked at him and there was a distant look in his eyes, a kind of sorrow that told me this was a very touchy subject. I let it go for now and looked forward to a lovely evening out with my new man.

We arrived at Trinkets & Art Delights to find it jumping with festivities: colorful lights were strung outside, a banner designed by the prima donna touting his face holding a palette and paint brush, smooth jazz music wafting through the night air, clinking of glasses, and loud laughter. I could tell that the guests must have started early on the champagne.

I held Hill's hand and we walked in like a celebrity couple, since the entrance was lined with red carpet, which I didn't approve, but must admit it added to the atmosphere. The only thing missing were the paparazzi. I shook my head and asked Tori who was standing at the door, whether the prima donna was inside.

"No," she said. "He just called and said 'I'll arrive when the artist within moves me.'"

"Have no idea what that means," I said.

Tori shrugged her shoulders. "Me neither."

"Oh, Tori, where are my manners? I'd like you to meet Hill Harris." Tori grinned as she extended her right hand to Hill and then said, "Nice to meet you."

"Same here. You've done a great job helping Deidre get this event off the ground," he said looking around at the lights.

"Thanks," Tori said, handing us a slender crisp sheet of white paper tied with a black bow at the top. "Well, here's the program for tonight as well as the listing of various art pieces and their prices."

"Thanks." Hill took the program and studied it for a minute before turning to me. "This guy must be awesome. Do you see these prices? They could break a brother."

"Wait till you meet him," I laughed, grabbing his arm. I led him into the front of the shop where the prima donna's art pieces hung from the ceiling and on easels which blended well with some of the shop pieces that were for sale. The shop was packed with people milling around with champagne glasses in their hands, laughing, chatting, and admiring the artwork.

"Come on let's mingle," I said. "Care for some champagne?"

"Maybe just one glass. I'm on call tonight."

"Hill, you didn't mention that. I was hoping to—" I whined.

"Hey," he said, kissing me softly on my lips. "I'll be here as long as you like." He jingled the car keys in front of me. "Remember I drove. Now how about that glass of champagne."

"Coming right up." I curtseyed before him in a polite gesture before I headed toward the make-shift bar in the back of the shop. While waiting in line to get served, I enjoyed the music and watched everyone having a good time. Suddenly, a familiar men's cologne surrounded me. *No it can't be. No it better not be. Gucci Rush.*

"Um, why don't you help someone else," I said to the bartender, turning around to face the man with the familiar cologne.

I pulled him to the side. "Kyle, what the hell are YOU doing here?"

"Glad to see you too, Deidre." His brown eyes rested on my chest. "Looking mighty hot in that dress tonight."

I tried not to blush. Kyle had a way of undressing me with his eyes that usually sent shivers down my spine. Seeing him tonight was no different, but I was here with Hill and didn't want to fall prey to his motives. I stared at him, still waiting for an answer.

Instead, he motioned toward Hill. "Is that your new arm piece?" "None of your business. I asked you a question. What... are...you...doing...here?"

"If you must know, I'm an investor in this art show. Thought I would like to see whether or not I'm going to make a profit. So here

I am."

I had to play it cool and not let him get to me. "Well enjoy the soirée and try not to cause any trouble. Can you handle that?" I asked in a snide tone.

"I'll try," he said, taking a sip of his drink.

Although he promised to be on his best behavior, I couldn't leave well enough alone. I was still pissed about him and LaTasha. "I see you left the hooker tramp at home. She doesn't present well does she?" I said, provoking him.

"Now that comment was not called for. I'm trying to be civil here. I promise I'll be good as long as you hold your tongue."

"Whatever."

"Hmm. You still have the jones for me don't you baby? That's why you're acting up. You could never hide your feelings very well. Must I remind you that you're the one who wanted this divorce, not me. I told you that I wanted to get myself together and you said no. I knew you would react the way you did because you bottled everything up until you exploded."

Kyle's words stung me. Despite everything we were a good fit, we worked well together, had similar taste in books, movies, the arts, and always had a great time on vacation. But his infidelity grew like a sore that would never heal and I needed to get away from it all before it drove me crazy.

"Here comes your new man." Kyle smirked as he put his arms around my waist.

"Kyle, let go of me." I pounded his chest, trying to squirm out of his grasp.

He grinned. "No. I'm not gonna let you go. I want to see how your new man is going to handle this." He held me tighter and then whispered in my ear, "Don't think I forgot about your late night call the other night."

Hill approached us before I could wiggle out of Kyle's grasp. I wish I had a drink to throw in Kyle's face but I didn't. I remained calm because I didn't want to cause a scene and ruin the evening.

"Am I interrupting something?" Hill looked at me and then at Kyle.

A nervous laugh escaped my lips. "Kyle, this is..." Kyle didn't budge, he kept holding me tighter. *Shit.*

"This must be the ex," Hill said, locking eyes with Kyle.

The man of my past and the man of my future. Two lions ready to pounce and I was caught in the middle. I had never been in a situation like this before and although I was sure some women would envy my position, it was a dangerous one to be in tonight.

Kyle continued holding me tighter. "And you must be her latest fling."

Hill didn't appear rattled by Kyle's comment. "My man, I think it's time you let go of the lady." Hill moved in closer to us. The situation was getting tense. I started sweating. They kept staring each other down. I was waiting for one of them to make a move and wreck the event.

Suddenly, Angela appeared. "Hey, hey good people. What's up? Deidre, you're needed up front, François, the prima donna is about to make his grand entrance." She put her hands on her hips, rolled her eyes and then snarled at Kyle. "So you gonna let her go or what?"

She stopped the disaster that was bound to happen between Kyle and Hill and I breathed a deep sigh of relief. Kyle smirked at her and then finally let go of me. I left both men still staring each other down when Angela pulled me away.

"Whew, thanks, girl. I swear I didn't know Kyle was going to be here tonight," I said, straightening out my dress and wiping my brow.

"Ain't this your place? You can tell his ass to leave."

"Yeah, but the prima donna rented the space and invited folks including his ass so I'm stuck."

"Damn, girl. Your life seems to get more interesting and crazier by the day."

"Tell me about it." I shook my head as I looked back at the two men: Mr. Past and Mr. Future and wondered what they were talking about. Hill stood at least two inches taller than Kyle. He had a cool head and I was confident that he wouldn't let things get out of hand if Kyle started to make a scene. It would be a sight to behold if these two came to blows. Kyle may be polished and soft spoken, but he was an avid boxer. Hill was a trained police officer and being from Brooklyn, I'm sure he'd had his share of fights. Not to mention when I was at his place, I saw championship trophies he had earned as a black belt in Tae Kwon Do.

"Girl, how do you manage to have these two men in the same

room?" Angela asked, licking the sauce from her fingers after eating a buffalo wing.

"Trust me, I didn't plan it that way. You think I'm crazy. One carries a gun and knows martial arts and the other boxes."

"Damn. Hill seems like an intense guy. Doubt if I'll get a chance to chat with him. I promised my daughter that I would get an autograph from the prima donna."

"I see the artist got you mesmerized too, huh?"

"Yeah, should be fun. Girl these hors d'oeuvres are the bomb. Gotta get the name of the caterer for when I plan my Christmas party," she said. "You sure love to eat," I laughed.

Angela eyed the server who passed by with an assortment of starters. "Uh-oh. Let me get that server. Didn't try the crab rangoon."

"Go right ahead."

"Hey, thanks for the invite. Enjoy Hill's company, here he comes. If I don't see ya then I know you're going to get some good loving tonight," Angela said as she chased after the server.

Hill walked toward me with two glasses of champagne. He handed me a glass and said, "I believe this is what you went to get at the bar before you got blindsided by your ex."

"Yup, thanks," I said, taking a sip of the bubbly. "What did Kyle have to say to you?"

"Brother got issues. Still thinks he owns you. But I set him straight."

"How?" I gave him a curious look.

"Told him you were your own woman and could make your own decisions about who you date."

"Yeah, that's right." My eyes sparkled at my hero. I didn't expect it but Hill kissed me on the lips in front of everyone. I turned to see Kyle's eyes turning green with envy. To make him even more jealous, I grabbed Hill's ears and pulled him in for a deep wet kiss.

"Mwah, there." I wiped extra lipstick from his lips and looked directly at Kyle who was still standing by the bar.

Tori stopped the music and announced that François was pulling up in front of the shop. Some of the guests began huddling closely together to peer out the windows, trying carefully not to spill their drinks; while others continued feasting on the flavorful hors d'oeuvres. Those who made it outside had their cell phones and digital cameras ready to capture this show-stopping moment.

"I guess François must be here. Now let's see this grand entrance," I said, turning to Hill.

"Where'd you find this artist who is so much into himself?" he asked, as he snuggled close to me.

"He found me and paid me handsomely to have this event. He's quirky, but hey, I don't mind."

"Wish he'd get on with it. The sooner we get out of here the sooner I can get you out of this dress. Hopefully before I get called into duty," he said, tracing his hands over the curves of my body.

Now that's a plan, I thought.

We all watched the black stretch hummer limousine that was parked out front and waited for the prima donna to grace us with his presence. Finally, after a few minutes, a tall chocolate, bald-headed man stepped his six-foot frame out of the limousine. He was wearing black combat boots, an unbuttoned long wool coat revealing a tight sweater framing his slender body with a motif-print scarf hanging around his neck. He tossed his head back, wrapped the scarf around his neck, raised his hands out to the crowd and announced, "People, I've arrived!" Guests snapped pictures of him as he greeted them and sashayed into the event.

Hill may not have noticed as he was busy caressing my legs, but someone had been following us since we left the art show. I kept looking in the side-view mirror for a while to be sure.

"You're awfully quiet. What's going on in that head of yours?" He reached over and gently tapped my forehead.

"Don't get into a fit, but I think we're being followed," I said calmly. He glanced into the rear-view mirror and kept driving. He didn't take my exit and instead kept driving on I-495. His cell phone rang.

"Aren't you going to answer that?"

He looked at the caller ID. "I guess I should, it's the station house calling. I'll get back to them in a minute. Let's see what this driver is up to." He kept driving and looking in the rear-view mirror, but the car didn't speed up or try to run us over.

After five minutes, the car turned off at a gas station.

"Oh well, I guess they were lost," he said.

I let out a sigh of relief. "I guess so."

He reached over and rubbed my shoulder with his right hand. My paranoia was getting the best of me. He then made his way back to Silver Spring and I relaxed in my seat. The station kept calling him and when he finally answered he told me he had to go in. I was disappointed, but I also understood that he had to handle a double homicide in downtown Baltimore. I was surprised that I was taking such a liking to a man in uniform. Police officers protect and serve, but I was never a fan of dating any of them until now. However, Hill managed to change the stereotype with his warmth and genuineness to help others. Like Kyle, he was still a workaholic but seemed willing to make time to be with me.

He walked me to the door. "Wish I could spend the night but duty calls."

"I understand," I pouted.

He raised my chin up to his eye level and then kissed me. "You're so beautiful. Thanks for a lovely and interesting evening," he said, putting his arms around me and rocking me from side to side. "Go lock up and I'll call you tomorrow. We still have to do that lunch, remember?"

"Yeah and I'm holding you to that Mr. Harris. Got a better idea, why don't you let me cook you dinner tomorrow evening if you're free?"

"A brother could eat."

"I'll take that as a yes. Be here by seven-thirty. G'night."

I blew him a kiss before I walked back inside. Through the peephole, I watched him climb into his car and saw the light in the front room go off in Ms. Benita's house. She must have been doing her late-night spying. Since I had been busy planning the art event and keeping late hours, I hadn't had time to see her and get the latest neighborhood gossip. I was still keyed up and needed to wind down.

I kicked off my heels, stepped out of my black dress, and peeled off my silk stockings on my way to the master bath. I threw my sexy bra and panty set that did not meet Hill's bedroom eyes and tossed them into the clothes hamper. I started filling the tub with hot water, poured in some lavender bubble bath, lit two Coconut Bay Yankee Candles, and then put on a Jill Scott CD. My body needed special attention, even if I missed the chance of getting it from Hill.

My cell phone buzzed with a text message from Hill.

"Wish I could be with you right now. Thinking of you. See you soon! - H."

His thoughtfulness brought a smile to my face. I stepped into the tub, laid back against the inflated pillow suctioned to the wall, closed my eyes, and pleasured myself.

CHAPTER 19

MY CELL PHONE RANG, STARTLING me at 8 a.m. *Who the hell was calling so early in the morning?* Without looking at the caller ID, I snapped, "Who the hell is this?"

"Whoa, Deidre. Chill out."

Shit. It was Hill. I quickly changed the tone in my voice.

"Sorry, Hill. It's so early and I wanted to sleep in today before doing the laundry and cleaning up the house."

"Guess, I should've spent the night, huh?" he asked in a sly tone.

"Humph, maybe I wouldn't be this grumpy. Forgive me?"

"Sure. Anyway you told me to call whenever I had a lead..."

"Uh-huh. What did you find out? Did you connect LaTasha to the murder?"

"Deidre, can I just speak?" he said sternly.

"Okay, let me shut up. Go on."

"Some Department of Public Works employees found a gun in a drainage pipe. They were fixing a water main break and—"

"Oh my God," I said, sitting up in bed. Hearing this made me excited that we may be a step closer to finding Lia's killer. Still, I wondered why I hadn't heard from Marcusetta. I was getting worried.

"Calm down. We might have caught a break, but ballistics still need to confirm that the shells we recovered at the scene were actually fired from the same weapon. Lia was shot with a .38 and the weapon the workers turned in was a .38 found very near the scene. I'll keep my fingers crossed that it's a match."

"Hill, the trial date for Taevon is coming up soon," I said.

"Yes, I know."

"If he sanctioned the hit on Lia then he could walk free if there is no other evidence in the case. Lia had to go out of town so she didn't have time to give a recorded statement."

"How do you know that?" Hill asked with curiosity.

Shoot, I ran my mouth. Now he knew that I had read the file. "Well...I...huh...read the file and called in a few favors at the clerk's office."

"It doesn't surprise me that you'd do that. From the first time we met, I knew you wouldn't stop at anything until you got answers." He laughed. "You should've been a cop. But seriously, remember there are rules and procedures. I'm sure you're aware of them."

"I know, I know. Can't help doing my own investigation...er, I mean asking questions. That's what they teach you on the job as a prosecutor. Ask questions, seek evidence, and find motives to get a conviction. The adrenaline rush can be quite addictive. This case brought it all back. Had no choice but to dig deep. I promise I won't break any laws," I said, crossing my heart.

"But, it's not over. You still gotta be careful."

"I know," I said in a low voice.

"So we're still on for dinner later?"

"Yup. See ya soon," I said excitedly.

After we hung up, I wondered why I hadn't heard from Marcusetta or Cassius about the address I asked him to check out. I didn't want to start fearing the worst and so I chose to remain patient until they called me. I needed to get my morning going and now that I was wide awake it didn't make any sense for me to lounge in bed. I tightened my bathrobe around my pajamas and headed to the front door to see if the newspaper boy did any better aiming for my doorstep. When I opened the front door, I bent down to get my paper and saw a yellow envelope sticking out underneath the welcome mat.

Sitting down in the love seat, I examined the envelope: no return address and my name was written gracefully in cursive. I slowly opened the envelope and pulled out the note. There were two sentences written with purple crayon:

"Leave my man alone! You'll be sorry."

It was written on stationary that looked custom made. I folded it and placed it back in the envelope. Could LaTasha have found out where I lived? Kyle didn't mention that she knew anything about me. Then again, he could be careless and talk if he had too much to drink. Could this be a warning to leave Hill alone? I recalled him saying that he wasn't dating anyone. Could he be lying to get some ass?

It wouldn't be the first time a man would say what he thought a woman wanted to hear just to get into her panties. This just added another layer of complication I wasn't ready to deal with today.

I unpacked the groceries and started prepping for my dinner date with Hill. I laid the chicken on the cutting board, rinsed, drained and chopped the collard greens, added spices from the spice rack, measured out some brown rice, and made a salad. Earlier, when I saw Ms. Benita in her driveway, I told her I was having Hill over for dinner and she offered to make him a banana caramel tart. I dropped off all the ingredients she needed to make the sweet treat I hoped to spoon feed him later that evening. I was still unnerved about the warning I had received this morning and wondered whether I should even tell Hill about it. I didn't want to spoil the evening, but I also wanted to use the time to find out more about the man I was spending time with. When I asked him about his brother, he clammed up. What was that about?

At seven-thirty sharp, I opened the door and found Hill holding a bottle of wine. "Hmm, I could smell the chicken roasting from the driveway," he said, handing me the bottle. "Didn't want to come empty handed."

"Something else your momma taught you boys?"

"Yes."

I stepped aside to let him in. "Make yourself comfortable. Dinner will be ready in a few minutes." I made a last min-ute inspection of the dinner table: it was draped with a white linen tablecloth with a red tablecloth over it, silverware, drinking glasses and wine glasses in their proper places to the left and right of the dinner plates, and a large red candle in the middle of the table with rose petals sprinkled around it. I stood back and admired my efforts. I had a Miles Davis CD playing in the background. The candle was lit. Perfect.

Hill crept up behind me in the dining room and remarked, "Girl, you went all out on this dinner. I'm a simple kinda guy. I was expecting something like lasagna or you passing off some KFC chicken as your own."

"Now you're funny. I wouldn't do that to the Colonel. Simple kinda guy, huh?"

"Let's just say it's nice to get a homemade meal every now and then."

"Well go ahead, have a seat."

"A brother is hungry." He inhaled the aroma of the roasted chicken and the collard greens as he laid the red napkin on his lap. "Hmm, can't wait to taste your cooking. Let me find out not only are you sexy as hell, but you can burn too. Wow! Now that's a combination and I must've hit the jackpot."

"Yeah, just hope I pass your test."

I served dinner and watched Hill devour the meal.

"That hit the spot," he said, wiping his mouth with the napkin.

The doorbell rang. "Hey, gimmie a second. That must be Ms. Benita, she offered to make you a special dessert. Be right back."

"That's very nice of her."

I opened the door, but no one was there. I looked down at the welcome mat and found another unmarked envelope. This time it was pink. I looked around but didn't see anyone. I was about to open the envelope when I saw Ms. Benita waving toward me.

"Evening chile. My you look purty tonight," she said, handing me the dessert.

"Thanks. That smells really good," I said, inhaling the caramelized flavor. "I wish I knew how to bake."

"When you're not too busy running around, maybe I can teach you some basic recipes."

"I'd like that. Hey, did you see anyone leaving my porch when you were coming over?"

"No, why?"

"Never mind."

"Well, it's still kinda warm, I hope he enjoys it. Saw the fella's car parked in your driveway and thought I'd bring it over now before y'all start some romantic stuff," Ms. Benita chuckled. "You got ice cream to go with it right?"

"Yes, ma'am. I remembered to pick up some vanilla ice cream, just like you told me."

"Well, all right then. Nighty-night!" She winked at me before heading back to her house.

I stood in the doorway and watched Ms. Benita disappear into her house before closing the door behind me. I rested the dessert on the glass-topped table next to the door and tore open the envelope. Same two sentences, same purple crayon, same message:

"LEAVE MY MAN ALONE! YOU'LL BE SORRY."

The only man here in my house is Hill so the message could only apply to him. *What timing!*

I tucked the envelope behind one of the throw pillows on the sofa in the living room before picking up the dessert and heading into the dining room. Hill sat back into his chair and patted his stomach. "Dinner was delicious. Can't believe your ex let you go."

"He's not interested in me and that's why we're not together anymore."

"I'm interested," he said in a serious tone.

I believed him, but until all the dust settled from this case, I probably wouldn't be able to fully take him up on that offer and see where this relationship was going. "Got room for dessert?" I said, switching the conversation.

"Yes. I could eat like this every day."

"Don't push it, Mister. Just wanted to show you a little appreciation. Glad you survived my cooking," I said, smiling at him.

"I'll eat this treat now and you later. Hope you got some whipped cream," he said, giving me a sly grin.

I cut two slices of the banana caramel tart and topped them off with a scoop of vanilla ice cream. "By the way, who knew you were coming here tonight?" I took a bite of the golden pastry and waited for his response.

"No one. Why'd you ask me that?" His brows furrowed.

"Ah, nothing." I decided not to harp on the notes and just enjoy his company. After dessert, he helped me clear the table and I poured us some wine to enjoy in the living room. I pulled out a photo album to show him some pictures of my family and friends. He stopped at a picture of Lia, Russell, and me when we went on a Halloween cruise at the Inner Harbor. Lia and I were dressed as wenches and Russell was dressed as a pirate wearing an eye patch over his left eye and a fake mustache curled up at the sides. In this picture, Russell held Lia around her waist and kissed her on her neck, his face shielded from the camera.

Hill stared at the picture before commenting, "This brother looked like he was having fun. I remember my brother and I used to play pirates and robbers when we were kids. He was the fun and adventurous one. I remember he used to get some of the girls in the neighborhood to play damsels in distress just so he would chase after them to steal kisses." He laughed.

"Yeah that's Lia's boyfriend, Ru—" The doorbell rang interrupting my response.

"Are you expecting company?" Hill asked.

"No." I was puzzled. "I'm sorry, Let me get that."

I opened the front door but no one was there. I slammed the door shut and stormed back into the living room.

"What's wrong? Are you okay?" he asked with concern in his voice. "Are you sure no one knows you were coming here tonight?" I looked at him sternly.

"Why don't you tell me what's going on?"

"It's weird, but I received two notes today warning me to stay away from 'my man.'"

"You sure they weren't talking about your ex?"

"Yeah, it wouldn't make any sense. Kyle and I are divorced so he's a free man. The only other man I could think of is you. I got the first note this morning and the second this evening before Ms. Benita brought the dessert over."

"Why didn't you tell me about it earlier?" He shook his head and held out his hand. "Let me see them."

I took the notes from behind the throw pillows and handed them to him. "I don't like playing games so I hope you're telling me the truth."

"I swear I live alone. I'm not seeing anyone. I have no scorned lover that would go psycho and want to hurt you. I told you that since Sierra died I was in a dark place romantically until I met you." His voice held a note of sincerity and I believed him.

We sat in the living room and he reviewed the notes. I could see the machines churning in his head when suddenly a look of concern washed over his face.

"What's wrong?"

"Nothing, can I hold onto them?"

"Why? Should I be concerned? Do you know who wrote them? What aren't you telling me?" I demanded.

Ignoring me, he got up and said, "I'll help you secure all the windows and doors before I leave. Then I gotta go."

I watched him walk out the front door without the notes. I was too perplexed by his behavior to clean up the kitchen. The romantic mood I had set went up in flames and I was left with many unanswered, burning questions, especially the reason behind his sudden departure. What the hell was really going on? It seemed like this was turning into a nightmare I wouldn't wake up from.

CHAPTER 20

E VERY SUNDAY WAS AN EVENT at Junction Baptist Church. There were two services, one at 8 a.m., which was more traditional and allowed members to enjoy a long afternoon, and the other at 10:30 a.m., which was more contemporary and for members like me who couldn't wake up in time to make it to the earlier service. I didn't feel like going to the 10:30 a.m. worship service, but Reverend Wright had left me a voicemail reminding me that I needed to be there. As I reluctantly got dressed, I reminded myself that I needed solace rooted in spirituality and would maybe get some clarity along the way.

Reverend Wright had been ministering at JBC for the past twenty years and had developed quite a following especially amongst the ladies, young and old. The younger ones would ask him for guidance about the young men and the older ones would constantly invite him over for special prayers at their homes, which he graciously declined. He was a very handsome man, with salt and pepper hair and a neat mustache. He had a welcoming boyish grin that put everyone at ease. Sometimes I thought if he weren't a man of God he would do well as a car salesman.

I walked into the lobby area and was immediately greeted by an usher wearing a black suit and white gloves.

"Morning sister, good to have you here today," she said, handing me a Bible, a hymnbook, and a program.

I thanked her and found an aisle seat in the back of the church in case I had to make a quick exit. I wished Hill were here with me, but he had left in such a hurry last night that I didn't get a chance to extend the invitation. I looked around and watched the members of the congregation: women in big fancy decorative church hats that blocked your view, pretending to be holier than others, but secretly wishing the Reverend would give them a special healing; men looking dapper in a colorful array of suits, eyeing the women—both married and single; and the crying children who were carted off to the nursery room by their mothers so that they could return to their seats to enjoy the service. Then I saw others who didn't miss a Sunday and genuinely came to hear the Word of God.

After the opening prayer and song, I felt more relaxed and waited for the Reverend to deliver his message. When he took the pulpit, he appeared regal in his black gown with kente stole. He scanned the congregation and his eyes rested in my direction when he saw me. His wife, who was seated up front, followed his gaze almost breaking her neck. When she saw me she quickly turned around and looked straight ahead. I shook my head, looked at the program, and marked the scripture reading in the Bible.

It never failed that whenever I attended church services the message was always geared toward me. Today, I was feeling down and the Reverend's theme of courage spoke directly to me. He asked everyone to turn to the book of Deuteronomy 31:6.

He read the scripture, *"Be strong and of good courage, do not fear nor be afraid of them; for the LORD your God, He is the One who goes with you. He will not leave you nor forsake you."*

He held onto both sides of the pulpit and then wiped the sweat from his brow after he jumped from one end of the platform to another delivering his message. The congregation was moved by the sermon and someone told him to preach on. One lady stood up, her eyes were closed and had her hand swaying back and forth to the music.

"Come one, come all, the Lord is calling you," the Reverend said as he called a special invitation to those who wanted to be saved. He stepped down from the pulpit and stood in front of the congregation.

"Have the courage to join Him today. Let me hear the church say amen!"

I remained stuck to the seat as a few people in my pew got up to go to the altar for this special calling. I watched as they sobbed their way to the front, repenting and asking for forgiveness. I closed my eyes and repented in silence.

At the end of the service, Reverend Wright greeted everyone with a hug and a hearty handshake at the door on their way to the repast in the hall area. "Rev that was a moving sermon," I said, hugging him.

He whispered in my ear, "I'm so happy you made it. Coming over for dinner?"

"I don't think so," I said, looking at the line behind me.

"Let's not hold up the line. Wait for me in my office. The door should be open. We'll talk there."

As much as I wanted to flee from the church after the service, my legs made their way to his office. When I walked in, I was greeted by the fresh scent of potpourri in a decorative glass bowl sitting on the side of his desk. The back wall was full of pictures of his family, celebrity ministers, certificates of appreciation, and his divinity diploma. It had been a long time since I sat in the Reverend's office. The last time I did, I was having problems with Kyle and he told me that all marriages have their ups and downs and that the true test was working through the rough patches. I listened, but the rough patches became major road blocks which were difficult to move.

I walked behind his desk, moved the curtain, and looked through the window. I saw his wife making her way to her car, but then she stopped and looked in my direction as if wondering why I was meeting her husband in his office. I closed the curtain, took a seat, and checked my cell phone for any messages while I waited for him. Hill still hadn't called. I sighed and tucked my cell phone away in my handbag.

It seemed like an eternity before the Reverend came to the office. The church was full this Sunday and he didn't like short changing the members with quick conversations and short hugs. He had to ask about the family and when they would bring a new member to visit.

So as I patiently waited, I thought about the Reverend's dinner invitation and decided that I was not in the mood to deal with his wife staring me down at the dinner table. To be honest, I wasn't sure if I could remain godly and not cuss her out. Finally, I decided to make up an excuse about dinner and hoped I wouldn't get struck by lightning in God's house.

The Reverend gently tapped on the door as he pushed it open. He donned a smile showing his pearly white teeth. He had a solid build for a man in his late-fifties and was very fit for his age.

"There you are. Thought you'd run out the back door when I wasn't looking," he said.

Little did he know I did consider that option. I smiled back.

He took a seat at his mahogany desk and steepled his hands. "Well, I didn't see your friend with you today. What happened?"

"He couldn't make it. But I showed up as promised. It was a good service and I hope you got some new members."

"Well, the choice is theirs. I'm only a vessel to bring forth the Word. But I was glad you finally came up for the community prayer. Thought you'd never move outta that seat." He laughed.

"Ah, what can I say." I shifted in my seat. "Rev, about dinner, I um..."

He stopped me with his hand. "It's okay. I understand. Instead of making up some excuse for not coming over for dinner, put me on your schedule when you're not too busy conducting your own investigation and we can have dinner just the two of us. Sounds like a plan?"

I marveled at how he could always guess my thoughts and my words. "You got me Rev, you got me. I can't wait to have a dinner date with you without the fuss. I'll let you know."

"Deidre, don't let this be your last visit. Come back to worship with the flock soon. Still need to meet this new fella of yours."

I smiled, got up and waved goodbye as I headed toward the door. I drove home with a renewed sense of courage, ready to see through the end of solving Lia's murder, ready to face off with Kyle about my hurt and anger and whether he had anything to do with Lia's murder, ready to confront Hill about rushing out and not wanting to face his demons, and ready to let go and find happiness again. I took a deep breath and felt a level of fearlessness I've never felt before.

CHAPTER 21

FRANÇOIS'S EVENT LAST FRIDAY NIGHT was a smashing success at least judging by the amounts of e-mails I had received when I came into the shop this afternoon. I was very pleased because some of the guests had requested some of the shop's pieces they saw on display at the event. I sent out a general response thanking them for their support and hoped they would come out to other events. I compiled an e-mail listing and sent it to Tori to make sure they received information for upcoming events.

Taking a break from reviewing invoices and other bills, I enjoyed the asiago roast beef sandwich I had picked up from Panera Bread on my way in. I hated eating cold food, but I was too hungry to complain. I took a sip of my soda and thought about Hill's behavior at dinner which left me unsettled. I hadn't spoken to him since he walked out of my house without an explanation and decided to shift my focus to work instead.

But as much as I tried, I couldn't focus because so many questions were left unanswered. I hadn't heard from Marcusetta or Cassius in a few days and even when I called Trixie she told me she hadn't heard from Cassius either.

"Deidre, I'm getting worried. He always checks in with me. I'm home more in the evenings and thought he'd be happy. But he's nowhere to be found," Trixie said.

"I'm getting worried too," I said, gathering up some invoices and putting them in my bag.

"Should I go to his house? He told me that the area is rough and that I shouldn't come around unless he's with me."

I nodded, *at least he was honest with her.* "Tell you what, I'll try calling Marcusetta again and see what I can find out. I'll call you soon. Sounds good?"

"Thanks, girl...I'm so worried about him," Trixie said with concern in her voice.

"It'll be okay. Call me if you hear from him. I hate to run but I'll catch you later."

Reaching for my car keys, I tried calling Marcusetta once again. This time the call went directly to voicemail on the first ring. Something was not right. I didn't tell Hill about my covert operation to get information on the house that I saw LaTasha go into when I followed her from Kyle's. Now I was on my way to Marcusetta's to see what was really going on.

When I pulled up in the side alley next to Marcusetta's house, I looked across the street at the blinking blue-light cameras, a reminder that this was a crime-ridden area under twenty-four hour surveillance. I grabbed my handbag from the passenger seat, opened it, patted my gun and got out the car. As I turned the corner, I saw Cassius's green Pontiac Bonneville parked in front of the house. My heart was going a million beats per second. Suddenly, I was startled by the buzzing sound of my cell phone. I looked at the caller ID, it was Marcusetta.

"Finally. I'm right outside your doorstep. Where've you been? Is Cassius inside?"

Marcusetta opened the door with the phone at her ear. "Well, come on in," she said, beckoning to me.

I ended the call as I walked up the steps. Marcusetta pulled me in quickly. I looked at her with concern. "What's going on? Haven't heard from you in a while."

"Keep your voice down. Cassius is resting." She grabbed my arm and led me into the front room. "Shhh. He got jumped a few nights ago and got beat up real bad."

My hands flew to my mouth. "Who did this? Did you call the police?"

"And say what? I tell you...those guys at the stash house didn't trust him when he came around asking questions." Marcusetta shook her head. "They tested Cassius."

"What do you mean?"

She paused and said in a low voice, "They wanted him to shoot up some drugs to show some loyalty even though he never ran with the crew."

I remained silent for a few moments before asking, "What did he do?"

"He can tell you himself."

I didn't press the issue with Marcusetta, but really wanted to know about LaTasha's connection to the crew.

"The woman I described to you. Do you know who she is?"

"Yeah, none other than badass LaTasha. I didn't realize it when you asked me about her but she's Taevon's sister."

"What?" I was astonished. "Do you know what she was doing at the stash house? Does she sell drugs too?"

"I know she's a stripper. My bad...exotic dancer. Same damn thing. Selling drugs, humph, don't know 'bout that. But she would do anything for her little brother."

"Would she kill for him?" I asked.

"Word on the street, she probably would. Since Taevon been on lock down, he's been giving her orders," Marcusetta said.

"I see. I guess Cassius got in the way and now he's all bruised up because I wanted to get some answers."

"He didn't go down without a fight. You should see some of dem other assholes."

"I was afraid this would happen," I said solemnly.

"It's cool though. I'm waiting for some of my homeboys to come up from North Carolina and then it's on. Cassius agrees with me on this."

Oh Lawd. "We don't need all that. Where is he? I need to talk some sense into him."

"Upstairs in the back room."

I climbed the stairs and knocked on the door. "Cassius, it's Deidre, may I come in?"

"Yeah," he groaned.

Pushing the door open, I found him sitting up in bed. His upper lip was busted up and he had bandages around his ribcage and his head.

"I'm sorry, I got you into this." I pulled up a chair and sat next to him. I held his right hand. "Tell me what happened."

His face grimaced with pain as he held the right side of his bruised rib cage. "I need a shot of Hennessey." He pointed to the dresser.

"You're a glutton for punishment aren't you? I should be giving you a glass of water and some painkillers, not this stuff," I said, handing him the bottle.

He took a swig from it and then took a deep breath. "That house is hot. Business is still jumping even though Taevon's in jail. Look like they celebrating too 'cause they say the prosecutor ain't have no case against him."

My heart palpitated. "Who said that?"

"One of his homeboys. Don't know his name though."

"What did they say about the drug bust and when Cuttie Banks got killed?" I asked.

"They 'bout to find out which joker did him in on the inside." He shook his head and took another swig. "It never ends. That's why I try to keep my nose clean. I gotta get away from all this nonsense. It's too easy for the po-po to pull up and hassle a brotha thinking we all the same, slinging drugs and doing crimes. I'm just a hard worker tryin' to live. I found me a girl and she's really feeling me. That's worth something."

"Yeah, I know. Which is why you should've called her."

"And say what, Deidre? That I went up into a stash house asking questions and refused to shoot up drugs in my arm and had to fight my way outta there." He hung his head low. "Nah, hell nah, couldn't do it."

"Look at me." I waited until his eyes met mine before I continued. "I spoke to Trixie earlier today and she's worried sick. Trust me, she'd understand. Just talk to her."

I wished I could take some of my own advice and just talk to Hill and come clean with everything I knew. I needed him and I'm sure he'd do what he could to shut down the stash house.

"Okay, hand me my pants," he said, pointing to them hanging over the ironing board. "I'ma call my boo. I hope she's not too mad at a brotha."

I smiled. "I'm sure she won't be. She'd be happy to know that you're all right. Tell her I said hey."

He smiled and I saw that he was missing a tooth that was knocked out during the fight. I promised him that I would cover his dental expenses before leaving his room.

Heading downstairs, the smell of fried fish filled my nostrils and made my mouth water. I went straight to the kitchen and saw Marcusetta dropping a piece of whiting fillet into the deep fryer while talking on the phone.

"What? Girl, he late again on da child support. Dat muthafucka." She covered the mouthpiece of the phone. "Hey Deidre. Hold on. Let me end this call. This bitch gossip too damn much."

"Sounds like the other way to me," I said laughing.

Marcusetta flipped me the bird and then ended the call.

"I have to run but tell Cassius that I'll have a police friend of mine reach out to him."

"You know we don't trust the po-po 'round here," Marcusetta said, holding the spatula in her hand.

"I know, but you can trust this one," I said.

"Well, if you say so. You staying for some southern cooking? Got some whiting fillet and some corn bread I'ma 'bout to throw down on."

I wanted to throw some hot sauce on the fish and fill my stomach, but I had to take care of some business. "Tell you what, make me a plate to go."

"Comin' right up," Marcusetta said, wiping her hands on a towel, then taking a plastic container from the top of the refrigerator and lining it with foil before putting the fish in. "Since you can't wait for the corn bread, I'ma give you two slices of white bread and some packets of hot sauce on the side." She snapped the lid shut and put it in a plastic shopping bag.

The scent of fried fish made my ride home difficult as I was tempted to open the container and break off a piece of fish and stuff it into my mouth. I decided to call Hill to make peace, even though I didn't think I had to. I couldn't afford to be stubborn and sit on this information.

After stopping to pick up my dry cleaning, I called Hill but the call went directly to voicemail. This was very frustrating, but I swallowed my pride and left a message:

"Hey, it's me. Gimmie a call. It's urgent, found out some interesting things about the case today."

I'd just gotten home and was about to unload the car when my cell phone rang. I juggled everything in my hand to get to the call.

"Sorry, I missed your call. How're you?" Hill asked.

"I'm fine, considering how you left the other night."

"I know. Been meaning to talk to you about that. Still got some issues and old wounds that need sorting out."

"I see. Are you sure you can handle the case and seeing me at the same time?" I asked.

"The case I can focus on, but sometimes being with you I could lose control. You're a special woman who deserves a man's undivided attention. Sometimes I get thrown off that's all. I hope I'm making sense," he said.

"I guess. Anyway, I followed LaTasha..."

"You did WHAT?" he shouted at me.

"I followed LaTasha the other day when she was leaving Kyle's and she went into a stash house in East Baltimore."

"You know for sure it was a stash house?"

"Yes. My friends Marcusetta and Cassius confirmed it. Cassius even got beat up trying to get some information for me. I want you to call him. He doesn't trust the police, but I told him he could trust you."

"I'm not even going to ask how...Tsk. Just give me the information."

The agitation in his voice didn't faze me. Now was not the time to address that issue. I gave him the address to Marcusetta's and told him that LaTasha was Taevon's sister and that they were celebrating that Taevon could get the charges dismissed against him. When I was done I waited for him to dig into me, but he didn't. Instead he went directly into cop mode.

"Let me reach out to Cassius. Does he have any ties to the crew?" he asked.

"No, he's just a hard working brother doing me a favor."

"I must say, you never cease to amaze me. You know some very interesting people willing to risk their lives for you."

I thought about it and nodded my head in agreement. "Yes, I do." "Well, let me get on this and see if I can set up surveillance on the stash house and the crew."

"Thanks, Hill."

"I hate to always run, but you know how the job is."

"Yeah, life of a homicide detective with very little down time." I thought, *could I live with that?*

CHAPTER 22

THE NEXT TWO DAYS WERE quiet. Too quiet. I wasn't used to sitting around twiddling my thumbs and I was getting fidgety. Hill had told me to be patient and that he would handle things, but I felt like I could be doing more.

As I was about to call Cassius, my cell phone rang and it was him. "You must be psychic!"

"Why?" he asked.

"I was just thinking about you. Did Detective Harris get in touch with you?"

"Yeah, he's cool peeps. Brotha different from the rest of the po-po."

"I know. So what's happening?"

"I told Trixie everything and she's been very cool about it. I don't know what I did to deserve this, but thank you for making the intro."

"I'm glad you two hit it off, but what's happening with the investigation?" "Homeboy says he's on it. He wants to move me somewhere safe. I told him nah, I would stay with my girl in Catonsville."

"I see. What's up with Marcusetta? She's still not willing to move out of the neighborhood?"

"Come on Deidre, you know how she rolls. I'm just glad I changed my mind and talked her into calling off her peeps in North Carolina. 'Cause it was about to be on like in that movie *Next of Kin* with Patrick Swayze. Did you ever see that movie?" he asked.

"Yeah," I laughed. "Didn't know you were such a movie buff...I know exactly what you mean. Guess I should stop worrying about her then."

"She'll holla at you if she needs anything. Right now you gotta be safe in case these clowns get froggy and want to leap."

"I hear ya. Glad I understand your lingo," I said.

He laughed. "Cool. A brotha gotta carry his weight in his woman's house, so I gotta go make dat bread. Be good."

After my conversation with Cassius, I called Marcusetta in a last-minute effort to convince her to leave the neighborhood.

"I fear no one," she said.

"Spoken like the true tough chick that you pretend to be," I said.

"If it's my time to go then so be it. I can't let them make me live in a box." Marcusetta's attitude punched me through the phone.

"That may be so, but I'm still afraid for you and your aunt."

"It's all good. They don't have nuthin' on me. Plus word on the street is that they are running outta juice."

"That's all that is, just word. Bet it won't take long for another crew to take their place. You should still leave," I said, trying my best to convince her. But it wasn't working.

"And go where? To the burbs? Back to North Carolina? Nah, don't think so. This is home, this is all I know. Plus my aunt believes the Lord will protect us," she said.

"You're so hard headed."

"Yeah, just like you. Maybe that's why we get along," she said.

I managed to chuckle, but I was deeply concerned for her and her aunt's safety.

"Just cover my boy and his girl. That's all I'm asking," she said in a serious tone.

"I will."

"We straight now?" she asked.

"Yes, we sure are. The only favor I'd ask would be for you to invite me over for some good southern cooking," I said laughing.

"Stop by anytime. Hey, can't chit chat with ya much longer, neighbor's here to get her hair did. Gotta go heat up that pressing iron," she said before rushing off the phone.

Looking at the calendar, I realized that there were only two weeks left before Taevon's trial and Hill still had no hard evidence. I prayed silently and hoped that they would find LaTasha soon because I didn't know what favor I would have to call in next if Taevon were to be a free man.

The investigation was picking up momentum. Hill somehow managed to expedite surveillance on the stash house and LaTasha. Undercover cops were posed as junkies hanging around the corner, search and seizure warrants were issued for the stash house and its occupants. I called Russell in Atlanta and told him about the latest developments. He was thrilled, but couldn't talk because he'd just taken a break from a musical performance and was due back on stage. I then called Lia's family and they were grateful that things were moving swiftly. Between the sobs during a conversation with Mrs. Reynolds, she thanked me for being a bloodhound on her daughter's case. I took that as a compliment. I became tenacious in tracking down leads despite Hill's constant warning to leave the detective work up to him.

This time I felt comfortable taking a step back until Hill called and told me that while the drug bust was going down, LaTasha was nowhere to be found. She'd managed to slip away when the officer assigned to surveillance fell asleep while waiting for his relief.

"How the fuck could that idiot fall asleep? He knew he shouldn't have let her ass out of his sight," he said angrily.

"Look, I'm pissed too, but I need you to stay calm. A cool head always prevails. You'll get her," I said, gritting my teeth and trying to heed my own advice.

"On top of everything..." he sighed heavily, "the bullet wasn't a match to the gun the DPW workers found."

My heart sank. I was hoping that it would point us in the right direction and this case could be wrapped up in a neat bow, but homicide cases weren't always neat. Sometimes, cases go unsolved for decades, but I didn't have that much time. "Dayum."

"Good news is it helped solve another murder we had on the books." There was a long pause on the phone. "Deidre, right now I don't need the wheels in your head to start spinning and you going off and doing something foolish. You've done great in getting us leads which would have taken us a long time."

"Guess we both need to practice some breathing techniques

to get through all of this. I'm sure you learned your share from your martial arts training or were your trophies fake?"

"They are real all right." He laughed. "See, that's why I need you, oh wise one."

"I know, I complete you." We both laughed.

"Wish me luck while I regroup the team," he said.

"Lots of it!"

Hill rushed off the phone and I hopped on my computer to read my e-mail messages. Within a few minutes, someone was furiously ring-ing the doorbell. I jumped out of my seat to see who it was. When I opened the door, Reverend Wright stood before me with bloodshot eyes, a noticeable five o'clock shadow, and wearing rumpled clothes. This was a far cry from the man who took command of his flock on Sundays, dressed impeccably, and in control.

"Rev, what's wrong? Come in, take a seat. Would you like something to drink?"

He looked at me with a seriousness I'd never seen before. "I need something strong."

"Got some brandy."

"That'll do. Bring two glasses. No ice."

"Coming right up," I said, looking at him quizzically before heading to the kitchen. *This must be serious.*

When I came back into the living room, he was sitting on the sofa shaking his head. I put the tulip glasses down, filled them with brandy, left the bottle on the table, and then sat beside him. I took a sip and waited for him to say something. Instead he picked up his glass, tilted his head back, and quickly gulped down its rich amber-colored con-tents. Whatever it was must have been serious because the strongest thing I'd ever seen him drink was the wine during the communion service. He filled his glass again before saying another word. Holding my hands, he locked his eyes on mine and then said, "Deidre, I want to talk to you about something."

"Uh-huh. What is it? Are you ill?"

"No, nothing like that." He placed his hand on top of mine and I grew apprehensive. "I, uh...don't know how to say this but..." He took a deep breath. "You're my daughter."

"I know Rev, I'm like the daughter you never had."

"No, I mean, you're my flesh and blood."

"What?" Shock and disbelief took over as I blinked my eyes to process what he had just said. "What do you mean I'm your flesh and blood? Huh, you and my mother?" I shook my head.

Now it made sense. For years I thought it was interesting how I would sweat on the tip of my nose and he would too. We had a similar sense of humor and shared a love for the outdoors. He would finish my sentences and knew what to say to comfort me, just like a father would comfort his own daughter.

He put his face in his hands, bent over between his legs, and bawled like a baby. I was crying too, my emotions mixed with anger and joy. Anger at my mother for not telling me the truth and joy I had found my real father and two half-brothers. I wasn't alone anymore.

He wiped away the tears from his eyes with the end of his shirt sleeve. When he composed himself he reached over and hugged me. "So sorry baby. I didn't know."

"How'd you find out?" I was curious.

"Well, it's a good thing you didn't come over for dinner after church because Ethel and I got into a big fight over you. She became enraged when I mentioned that I had invited you over for dinner. I'd never seen her like that before." He clasped his hands. "And that's when she told me that years ago, your mother had sent a letter addressed to me before she died telling me that I was your father. Ethel kept the letter hidden in the attic with the rest of her stuff and then changed into an angry bitter woman overnight. I couldn't figure out why."

"What did she do?" I pressed.

"She cut me off in the bedroom for a long time. She didn't go to church for several Sundays which left many tongues wagging. When she finally realized that the gossip was growing she threw me a life line, started going to church, inviting me back into the bedroom, but things were never the same." He paused. "Somehow I always felt a special connection to you. I wanted to tell you in person, not over the phone. I didn't know how you'd take it and I didn't want to lose you."

"Well, this is quite a shocker but I'm thrilled. Wow, you and mom. Thought you two were just great friends. Whoever said that men and women can be just friends should stop kidding themselves."

"Amen to that."

"What happens now with your wife?" I asked.

"She seemed relieved that she's unburdened this secret she had hidden from me. Not much I can do now. I apologized to her. It was a moment of weakness, but I've remained faithful since then."

"How did you and my mother hook up?"

"Your mother called me over one night. She'd found a pair of lace panties in her husband's pants pocket when she went to do the laundry, and she flipped out."

He finished his second drink before continuing. "She was crying and very distraught. I couldn't let her be alone. I came right over and one thing led to another." He shook his head. "I'm a man, it's no excuse, but I was weak. We never spoke about it again because we were both married. If things were different I would've married your mother in a heartbeat." A moment passed by before he said, "I loved her." And we drank to that.

CHAPTER 23

I SAT IN FRONT OF THE TV and watched the news as reporters swarmed East Baltimore with microphones, notepads, and cameras ready to capture the raid on the stash house. The drug bust played out surreally like a gangster movie: Taevon's crew members were handcuffed and escorted into police vans, mountains of drugs, arsenal of guns, and brown bags of cash were carted out of the stash house. When LaTasha left town, there was no leadership in place and the crew was operating on its own. They got sloppy, their defenses were down and now they all faced multiple felony charges.

I felt relieved, but could not rest easy until I knew LaTasha was caught. While I was glued to the TV, Hill called me from the drug bust.

"Deidre, we found it!" he said excitedly.

"Found what?"

"The gun. Could be the murder weapon."

"Where?"

"It was wrapped up in a T-shirt and hidden behind a wall in the kitchen."

"Sure hope it's the evidence that ties LaTasha to the murder," I said.

"Told you I was on a mission. We tore that house up. We even had the K-9 cops sniff out the drugs. Now that we've found the gun, all we gotta do is tie LaTasha to it. Hold on, got another call coming in," he said.

"Call me when you catch that..." A series of gun shots interrupted the call. One camera man was brave enough to keep the camera rolling until the TV station cut to commercial.

My hands flew to my mouth. "Oh my God, Hill."

Ten minutes later, my cell phone rang. It was Hill sounding out of breath. "Hey, did you hear that?"

"Yes, what happened? Are you okay?"

"Whew, that was close. I'm okay. SWAT missed one of Taevon's crew members when they went into the house. They were loading the others into the police vans when he came out with guns blazing at us. It was like a gunfight at the O.K. Corral. I had to take cover behind one of the
squad cars."

"That must've been terrifying."

"Yeah, we had to take him out," he said.

"Guess I won't be seeing you anytime soon, huh?"

"Not tonight baby. Too much to do," he said, sighing heavily.

"Any word on LaTasha?"

"Still in the wind and nobody's talking. But we'll see when we get these thugs to the station unless they lawyer up."

"I'm just glad you got the drugs and guns off the streets," I said.

"Every day is a war and we can only win it one battle at a time."

"How poetic."

"I can get deep sometimes," Hill chuckled.

"Promise me you'll be safe. Oh and I have some wonderful news to share with you, but I want to do it in person."

"Okay. Can't wait to hear all about it. Hope it involves you getting naked, me handcuffing you to the bed, you wearing your red sexy high heels, and me massaging you with some body oil."

"You're so freaky! But no, nothing like that but if you play your cards right you might get lucky."

Over the next few days Taevon's entire crew showed solidarity in not saying a word about their leader and LaTasha. I was beginning to fear that LaTasha would remain a fugitive until I got a call from Hill which turned things around.

"Great news. I'll be heading to Philly to follow up on a lead from an anonymous tipster about LaTasha. The funny thing is this person would only talk to me about it."

"That's weird. I hope it's not an ambush," I said.

"Thought about that, but it seems legit. We're going in strapped and with a lot of eyes so it should go down smoothly."

"I hope so. You never know what to expect these days with folks wielding guns. You know she is not wrapped too tight, so be on guard."

"You really do care," he said, slightly above a whisper.

"Ah, guess I do. I want you back in my arms without a scratch on that fine ass body of yours."

"Now you're talking. It's been a while since I tasted you."

I envisioned what he'd do to me with his gifted tongue and my panties became wet at the thought of being with him again. "Mmmm."

"Keep it warm for me. I'll need to unleash some of the adrenaline I've been running on for the past couple of days."

"I'll be wetty," I said.

"That's what I love about you woman, you're funny."

In the background, someone shouted "Hill gotta go man. Get your gear!"

"Go. I'll see ya soon," I said, silently praying that he'd return to me safely.

Several hours later, Hill called me on his way back to Maryland and filled me in on LaTasha's arrest. He told me that when the Philly PD got to the house where they suspected she was staying, an undercover officer pretended to hand out flyers for an event at the local bar. They spoke to a woman wearing an oxygen mask over her nose and mouth, who identified herself as LaTasha's mother. She told them that her dutiful daughter had made a trip to the corner store to buy her some cigarettes.

The police staked out the house and waited for LaTasha to arrive. When she showed up, she immediately started exhibiting behavior of a crazy woman: ranting and raving, pulling on her hair, tearing up her clothes, kicking and screaming until she was taken away in handcuffs. After she calmed down, she waived her right to an attorney and confessed to everything in the squad car.

"Just like that she confessed?" I was shocked.

"Yup, she said she shot Lia and that she acted alone. Taevon had no idea about the shooting," he stated.

"Did she say why?" I asked.

"She said she wanted Taevon to get out of jail and be free to reclaim his kingdom on the streets. She said she was tired of the drug game and just wanted to be with your ex. Humph, seems to me like she was handling things well at the stash house," Hill commented.

"What did she have to say about shooting Kyle?"

"She said she didn't know it was him when she started shooting. She thought he was some random person who could've identified her."

"So she kept her mouth shut when she found out she had shot him."

"She sure did," Hill said.

"That bitch is nuts! Bet she's gonna try to plea insanity to the charges."

"She may very well try to do that. But we'll see. One thing is certain though..."

"What's that?" I asked.

"She's crazy about your ex."

"Really? Never mind about that. What else did she confess to?"

"She said she gave the order for Cuttie to jump you in front of your house and to chase you on the highway. He was also the one who left you those threatening text messages. I guess she felt you were too much on her trail and wanted to scare you off."

"Damn. Wish I could beat her ass to a pulp right about now."

"Now who needs to calm down?" Hill asked.

"Sorry. This whole thing was just too stupid. My best friend lost her life because she wanted to do the right thing and this is how she gets repaid. So could Taevon walk away from killing the shop owner?"

"No. We lucked up, another witness came forward after seeing that the crew was arrested. Guess they felt there wouldn't be any retaliation now."

"This is the society we live in. At least someone decided to do the right thing by stepping forward," I chimed in.

"I know. Deidre gotta tell you something else."

"Do I really need to hear it? Fine. What is it?" I was getting exasperated with all these revelations.

"Um, LaTasha also ranted about your ex abandoning her when she needed him the most," he said and then he paused. "She also has twin daughters and claims your ex is the father."

This information knocked the wind out of me. I wasn't prepared to hear it, although it was a strong possibility that it could have happened given his track record of being a philanderer. "Have mercy. Ain't that some shit. He's such an asshole. Bet he'll lie about that too."

"There's more," he said.

"Ah, what else?" I was growing weary.

"I think your ex may have been the anonymous tipster," he said.

"How do you know that?"

"Call it a hunch. The desk officer said it was a very arrogant male who wouldn't leave a message and that he'd talk to no one but me."

"Mmm-hmm, that sounds like him. At least he finally did something right."

I wondered why the sudden change in Kyle. When I told him that LaTasha could've murdered Lia and then shot him, his reaction told me that he had no clue that he was sleeping with the enemy. Knowing him, he was probably on the run for fear she would put a hit out on him. That's his problem now. I was done with him and finally ready to move on with my life, but I made one last effort to reach out to him.

I picked up the phone and called all the numbers I had for him and got no response. Despite the late hour, I jumped in my car and drove all the way to Fell's Point. When I arrived at his townhouse, I saw a For Sale sign in the window. I peeked in and the house was empty. I sat in my car and hoped wherever he was, he was free from harm. Was I nuts for still caring?

CHAPTER 24

⌒

THAT NIGHT I WAS SO mentally exhausted that I drifted off to sleep without turning on the alarm. I dreamt that I was drowning and frantically tried to save myself. I struggled to come up for air, but something kept holding me down. The dream felt so real that I began to open my mouth to suck in some air. I thought I was still dreaming until I couldn't move my arms. When I opened my eyes, a dark figure was kneeling over me pinning my hands down. *This can't be.* The dream had now become a living nightmare.

I tried to scream, but a hand covered my mouth. I squirmed under the assailant's weight, but he was too strong. I felt something silky was being tightened around my neck. I tried to wrestle his hands away from my throat.

I wasn't about to lose my life in my damn house not when I'd just found my real father and a new love. NO FUCKING WAY!

I didn't know where the strength came from, but I managed to knee whoever it was in the nuts. He fell to the floor doubled over in pain. I quickly spun over to the nightstand drawer and grabbed my gun and rolled back to the center of the bed. He stood up and lunged at me, trying to get a hold of my legs, and that's when I fired three times—hitting him in the upper body. The body fell to the floor with a heavy thump.

"I got you now, you bastard." I leaped off the bed and kicked the body. There was no movement. I turned on the lamp to identify my assailant, who was dressed in all purple, and wearing a mask. I laid the gun down on the floor and my hands were trembling as I yanked off the mask to reveal a face that looked quite familiar, but it didn't make sense.

"Sierra?"

The assailant had breasts, but the hands were huge, the body was heavy, and I'd kicked the person in the nuts.

I blinked. "Sierra? No, this can't be?"

I stood over the body in a state of confusion. I picked up the gun from the floor and held it by my side. I stepped over the nylon stocking and the serrated knife the assailant had intended to use to end my life. Before I could pick up the phone to dial 9-1-1, I heard Ms. Benita shouting and banging on the front door downstairs.

"Deidre, you all right in there? Open up." More banging on the door. "Whoever is in there don't hurt that poor chile. The police are on their way."

"I'm okay!" I shouted as I bolted for the bedroom door.

Suddenly, the assailant grabbed me by my hair and tried dragging me back into the room. I fought back and this time I managed to kick him in the shin. His knees buckled and then I shot him right between the eyes. He fell to the floor, face first with a loud thud.

I was breathing heavily by the time I made it downstairs. My heart was beating fast as I flung the front door open. Ms. Benita stood there, terrified and gripping her baseball bat.

"Oh my God. What happened in here? Are you okay? I heard gunshots coming from your place and called 9-1-1. We need to get outta here," Ms. Benita said, pleading with me.

My feet couldn't move. Ms. Benita instinctively embraced me and then led me to the sofa. No words came; I was still in shock and pointed upstairs to the bedroom. Leaning the baseball bat against the sofa, she held me around the shoulder to steady my trembling body. "I'm not going up there." Looking at the gun, she said, "Put that thing away before you shoot me too."

I gently placed the gun down on the coffee table. "I'm too drained. Let's just wait here until the police show up."

"Chile, I'm not leaving you, but I sure hope you killed whoever it is upstairs 'cause I don't want to have to hurt nobody," she said, wrapping a blanket around my shoulders.

"I sure hope so," I said. "I wish the police would hurry up."

"I don't know what kind of trouble you're in, but I sure hope this is the last of it. Deidre, it's just too much for one person to handle," Ms. Benita said.

I agreed with her. "Thanks for being here. What would I do without you being such a snoop?"

Ms. Benita smiled. "Like I always said. I'm just doing my civic duty." I heard the wailing sounds of the police and ambulance entering the neighborhood and knew I was in for a long night of questioning.

"Do you want me to call your police friend?" Ms. Benita asked.

A faint smile came across my face. "Yes. Here's my phone. He's listed under 'Protect and Serve.'"

Ms. Benita made the call and told Hill that I didn't have the strength to go into the entire matter over the phone. "She's too shaken up. She just shot somebody. Just get here as fast as you can. Time's a wasting!" she told him.

At two in the morning, I could only imagine that the neighbors were across the street in their pajamas, housecoats and bedroom slippers gawking at the scene. This time, I'd shot and killed someone.

Ms. Benita looking out the window said, "Unbelievable. Look at these people staring over here."

"Ms. Benita, you're one to talk. You know you'd be the first one out there if it were someone else," I said.

"You're right. Anyway, chile I need to fix me a drink. This is too much drama for me."

"Bring me one too," I said, massaging my temples with my fingertips.

When the paramedics arrived, they wrapped me in more blankets and checked all my vitals.

"Ma'am, you've just experienced a traumatic event. You're in shock. You need to come with us to get checked out at the hospital," one of the paramedics said.

"No, I'm good. You said my vitals are fine, I just need to rest."

"But—" the paramedic insisted.

"I *said* I'll be fine."

"Well, we can't force you to come with us," he said, walking away and going over to his partner.

I hardly had time to breathe before the detective approached me with his notepad and pen ready to take my statement about the shooting. I told him I'd gone to bed and forgotten to turn on the alarm system. Then someone was trying to strangle me with nylon stockings. I fought back and then eventually shot and killed him. I told him I had no idea who the assailant was or why he'd want to hurt me. These questions went on for a while until Hill arrived. He flashed his badge and walked toward me. I was still shaking, but calmed down once I laid eyes on him. I'd never killed anyone before, but tonight it was either him or me and I had to survive.

"What the hell is going on?" Hill asked.

"And thanks for asking how I'm doing?"

"I'm sorry. I thought all this mess with Taevon was over and that you'd be safe. Who would want to hurt you now?" He hugged me. "Sorry, baby. Are you okay?"

"I'm fine. Just a little shaken up, that's all." I didn't mention to Hill that the person I had shot and killed looked a lot like his deceased wife. This was all too puzzling.

The forensics team was still upstairs working on the crime scene: taking pictures, logging, tagging, and packaging evidence. When the coroner's team came downstairs with the victim, Hill stopped them to take a look at the body. As soon as he unzipped the body bag, his knees caved under him, he fell to the floor, his hands flew to his head and he let out a wail so painful I felt it through my bones. "Noooo."

"Man, you all right?" an officer asked, resting his hand on Hill's shoulder and then helping him to his feet.

He mumbled a few words which I couldn't hear.

I walked over to him, "Is she—?"

He said sadly, "It's not a she, it's a he."

"Huh? I saw breasts and...huh...I kneed the person in the groin."

"It's Stephan, Sierra's twin brother!" he said.

"What the fuck? A tranny with boobies and a dick? What the hell was *he/she* doing in my house?" I shouted.

He sadly shook his head. "Damn. Can't believe he's the Moonlight Strangler."

"What? This motherfucker followed you all the way from New York? What kind of crazy shit is this? It doesn't make any damn sense," I said angrily.

Hill looked at me. "It does now. The stationary those notes were written on were from Sierra's private collection. She designed them. She used to write me love notes and put them in with my lunch. The box of stationary was missing on the night of her death. When I saw it, I panicked and couldn't believe that whoever took them from my house would end up in Maryland and at your doorstep."

"And you didn't say SHIT to me!" I snapped.

"I was still gathering information."

"That's all you can say. Still gathering information." I fumed.

"I know you're pissed, but I needed to be sure. I called up to Brooklyn to see if there were any other killings reported. And you always had your alarm system on so I wasn't very worried."

"Well just my luck. I didn't turn the alarm on tonight. I could've been killed." A tear slid down my face. I pummeled his chest with clenched fists. "I could've been killed."

"And I couldn't live with myself if that had happened." He held me close to his chest. "I'm so sorry. Please forgive me."

I sobbed in his arms for what seemed like an eternity until the detective asked whether I had a place to stay. Hill turned to him and answered for me.

"Detective Wilson, I got this. She'll be okay," he said.

I was drained and ready to get away from all this madness. I wiped my nose with a tissue. "Why? Why me?" I sobbed. "You need to make this make sense."

"Stephan always told Sierra that he had the hots for me but I didn't swing that way. I didn't find his confession to her funny and I told her he couldn't come around the house when I was there. I told her that if he tried any bullshit with me, I would kick his ass. I guess his fantasy of him being with me and playing house drove him crazy and he killed my wife, his own sister. That crazy son of a bitch!"

"That explains why he killed Sierra but why the other victims?" I asked.

"I need to check into that, but I'd bet he fell for those women's husbands or boyfriends and he received the same rejection and thought if he took the women away, the men would love him."

"What's with wearing purple and using a purple crayon to write the notes?"

"Believe it or not, he's an art instructor and purple is his favorite color."

"That's some sick crazy shit!" I said vehemently.

"I know. That's enough for tonight. Let's get you outta here," he said. "I need to get a few things for my overnight bag."

"Pack enough for a week. It'll be some time before you'll be able to get back into the house."

"Ain't this some shit," I said, looking around my house at the yellow tape going all the way up to my bedroom.

"Never a dull moment with you, huh Deidre?"

"Nope. Now can I get some help? And I need to call my father," I said, reaching out for him to help me up from the sofa.

Hill looked at me strangely. "Thought you weren't in contact with your father."

"Not that man in California. My real father...Reverend Wright. We'll talk about this later."

I told Ms. Benita to keep an eye on my place until I could find the courage to come back. I planned on calling my father, Angela, and Tori and telling them what had happened, but that could wait until later in the day, unless they saw my drama on the news.

I spent the entire afternoon in bed. I ached a little, but Hill took great care of me. He had someone take his shift and spent the day with me. I was still reeling from last night's events and was thankful that I dug deep to get through it. Hill was relieved, but still couldn't get over the fact that Stephan followed him all the way to Maryland to win him over. He called his former police precinct in Brooklyn and confirmed his suspicions that Stephan knew the husbands and boyfriends of the other victims and that Stephan had made passes at them which they rejected.

Hill told me that the police searched Stephan's apartment in Brooklyn and found the following items: a gold watch from the first victim, a gold brooch from the second victim, a gold ring from the third victim, and a gold locket which he gave Sierra on their first wedding anniversary. Taking the stationary was just an added bonus. All these items were reported stolen or missing from the victim's home and were found hidden in Stephan's house.

"Why did he only take gold items?" I asked.

"Funny you'd ask that but he'd always tell us that wearing gold gave him a sense of power," he said, sitting on the edge of the bed and putting on his shorts. He sighed heavily and then said, "I guess that's the end of the Moonlight Strangler."

"Thank God for that! Now you can give me your undivided attention," I laughed. "Where're you off to now?" I asked, propping myself up on one elbow and reaching around him to play with his curly chest hairs."

"Station house called. Gotta go in, something about Marvin running an illegal gambling operation at the Kitty Kat Club and someone getting shot."

"Humph. I'm glad Trixie got out of there. That place was trouble."

"And my work never ends." He lifted my hand from his chest and kissed it. "Are you gonna to be okay when I leave?"

"Don't have much of a choice do I? Go ahead and go. I should be pretty safe here."

"You sure?" He turned, holding my shoulders and looking into my eyes.

"Yes, I'm sure. You have cable don't you?"

"Yup, all the premium channels and more than you can handle. Order a movie if you like."

"Don't mind if I do," I said. "Hand me the remote please."

He handed me the remote and kissed me on the forehead. "Be back as soon as I can. I hope this is it. I can't wait for things to get back to normal for you."

"Yeah, it's been such a blast," I said sarcastically.

"See you later when I get home. That has a nice ring to it. Don't you think?" He laughed.

I heard him walk through the front door. I felt right at home at his place and relaxed in bed. I checked my voicemail which overflowed with messages: several from my father and Angela, worried about me because they saw the news; a few from Lia's mother crying that she almost lost me; one from François, the prima donna asking when he could do another exhibit; one from Tori saying that I had missed a meeting with another artist who wanted to have a nude sketch party. I shook my head at the last message from Kyle.

"When was the last time I heard your voice? Tasted you? Felt you? Heard you moan?

I swear he must be on drugs. He cursed me out the other day and now wanted to taste me.

Click.

CHAPTER 25

LOOKING OUT MY WINDOW, I watched the snowflakes fall-ing to the ground. Winter was officially here and the dust from all my drama had finally settled. I had much trepidation about going back to my house after the Stephan incident, but Hill helped me ease back into sleeping in the master bedroom. We had been spending more time together and getting to know each other. I'd told him about the Reverend and the circumstances how he found out that I was his daughter. He was blown away by the story, but happy that the Reverend was in my life. He told me about his brother that he hadn't seen in several years and that he missed him.

I snuggled deeply into Hill's arms after our early morning sex mar-athon in my queen-sized bed. He was an attentive lover and I loved that about him.

He tongue kissed me deeply. "Can I get some more?" he asked as he sucked on my breasts.

"I don't know where you're getting all this energy but a sister gotta rest. I know it's your birthday weekend and all but save some for later," I said teasingly.

"Okay, okay. You're lucky I'm digging you something fierce," he said. "Ha, ha and for the record, I'm digging you something fierce too, so...I guess we're just digging each other."

"Agreed!" He laughed.

I got up from the bed when my cell phone rang. It was my dad. Once he told his sons that I was their sister they were readily on board. It made sense to them now why their mother always acted strangely toward me whenever I was around. Like their father, they were easy going and couldn't wait to spend some quality time with me to officially welcome me into the family.

"Hey Pops. What's up? What's on your agenda for today?"

"The boys want to hang with their Pops today. Care to join the family?"

"Another time. I'm here with Hill and plan to spend the entire day in bed?"

"TMI. I know I'm your father, but some things I really don't need to know," the Reverend said.

"Sorry Pops," I said lightheartedly.

"So does Hill know about his surprise birthday party this evening? What time do you want us to get there?"

"Hold on." I stepped into the bathroom and shut the door. "I'm back. Didn't want Hill to know what was going on. Um, seven-thirty should be fine. Tori will get you seated and we should get there by eight. I'll tell him that we have another pretentious event to attend at the antique shop."

"That sounds like a good plan. You sure he doesn't suspect anything?"

"Pretty sure. Remember Russell?"

"Yeah, artsy dude with the dreadlocks, Lia's boyfriend. I remember him."

"I called him last week and he promised to perform at the party. I'm so excited. He'll finally get to meet Hill. He's been nagging me about giving him details about the new man in my life, but I told him it would be a surprise."

"That's great! Hill's a cool dude. I like him." The Reverend had met Hill when I took him to church several Sundays ago. They hit it off and even spent some time working in his home garage on a few vintage cars. This had become Hill's latest hobby and he couldn't wait to get his hands dirty fixing these cars when he had some down time. This made my father very happy since his sons were in living different states and only came home for the holidays.

"Will the boys stick around for the party or do they have other plans? I know how they get when they come to town. They have to see all their homeboys, hang out at the clubs and whatever else they do," I said.

"Wish they would cut out some of the drinking and clubbing. But they're grown. Not much I can do about that. Not to worry, we'll be there even if I have to twist a few arms to get them there," my father said.

"Cool! Oh damn, sorry Pops but look at the time. Russell will be arriving soon at BWI airport and I gotta go pick him up."

"You better get going and drive the speed limit. I know you have lead for feet."

"Ha. Ha. You're getting to be just as funny as Hill."

"Just a friendly reminder that's all. Oh and we're all set for Russell to stay with us after the performance tonight," he said.

"Look at you getting all hip. Let me get outta here. Looks like I'm picking him up at the Delta Terminal and then taking him to the shop to set up. Hope I don't have to move my car before the airport rent-a-cops see me. You know how they get if you're parked too long out front."

"They're just doing their jobs, baby. See you and Hill later. Hope you got some good food that will stick to the ribs, not those vegetable and cheese trays," my father said.

"Oh, I got it all hooked up!"

Another spectacular event at Trinkets & Art Delights. This time I had a special occasion planned: Hill's birthday celebration. I had postponed the prima donna's request for this month, but I wasn't a fool to let his money slip through my hands. So I rescheduled his event for next month. Tori prepared everything on schedule, including getting the same caterer from the prima donna's first red carpet event, the decorations, and stocking the bar for the bartender. All I had to do was get Hill to the shop without blowing it.

"My, my. You sure are working that *Armani* suit." I eyed Hill seductively.

He gently slapped me on my ass as I walked away to apply my makeup in the bathroom. He followed me inside, kissed the nape of my neck and whispered, "Can't wait to have you tonight as topping for my birthday."

"You can do whatever you like, birthday boy!" I said naughtily.

"That's what I like to hear. You do so much to make me happy," he stated.

"I know you'd do the same for me too. Anyway, hope you don't mind the prima donna and his shenanigans. If he gets to be too much over the top we'll leave and go somewhere quiet for some drinks and then it's on."

"I can't wait. I had so much fun the last time I wouldn't miss it. Hope your ex doesn't show up again," he said, eying me mischievously.

I hadn't thought about Kyle for some time, but now that Hill had mentioned him, I wondered whether he was well or not. "I'm sure he won't be there."

When we arrived at the shop, the parking lot was full, but Tori made sure that I had a reserved space. Hill opened the passenger side door, took my right hand, and eased me out of my seat. As soon as we walked through the front door, the entire room erupted singing Happy Birthday. Hill was totally surprised as he looked around the room and saw most of his friends from the force, including those from his squad in Brooklyn.

"How'd you manage this?" He looked at me in amazement.

"I got skills, brother."

He drew me close to him and kissed me. "Thank you, baby. This has been the best birthday present ever," he said whispering in my ear.

We took our seats at the table decorated with balloons designated for the birthday boy.

The lights dimmed and the sounds of strumming and picking of guitar strings stilled the room. Russell was sitting on a stool with his back turned to the audience who were waiting in anticipation. The sounds developed into a soulful rhythm, one that transported you to another place. Whenever Russell played, he would hang his head down near his guitar and groove to his own sound. Tonight, he sported a bandana tied around his dreadlocks which was a very different look for him. He wore a black vest over a white shirt unbuttoned to his chest. His jeans were torn at the knees and he wore loafers without socks.

When Russell turned around and looked out into the audience, I saw a startled look on Hill's face. It was as if he had seen a ghost. He blinked his eyes twice. "No-uh. No way... Heath?" Pointing at the stage, Hill exclaimed, "Deidre, that's Heath my brother!"

I was surprised by Hill's reaction to Russell, whom he thought was his brother Heath. "No way. You must be mistaken. That's my friend, Russell. Lia's boyfriend," I said, nudging him.

"I'm telling you baby, I'm not mistaken. That's my brother Heath. I could pick him out anywhere in a crowd."

"Oh my gosh!" I was stunned. Hill stood up from his chair and was about to get closer to the stage when I held his hand. "Wait, wait until he's finished with his songs."

Hill sat and enjoyed the music that his brother played. After the first set, Russell stood up, swung his guitar around his back and took a bow. The applause was loud, the crowd loved him, and a few whistles were heard. I walked up to the stage and took the microphone from the holder.

"Let's give it up for Russell Hilson. He came all the way from Hotlanta to play for this special occasion." I started clapping.

Another round of applause erupted and Russell took another bow. His brows were heavy with perspiration from sitting under the hot spotlight. I turned to him and said, "Thanks so much for coming out to my man's birthday party."

"Yeah, no problem, sister." He gave me a hug. "So when do I get to meet this mystery man of yours?"

"Right now." I took his hand and we stepped off the stage and headed toward Hill. As we got closer, the look on Russell's face confirmed the connection between him and Hill. Tears welled up in his eyes as he let go of my hand and rushed toward Hill. The two men embraced each other in a warm brotherly hug and they both pointed at me for a group hug. I was choked up.

Russell was the first to speak, "Deidre, I knew there was some cosmic energy in this place tonight. The energy was just right." He turned to Hill. "Bruh, I know you're gonna cuss me out but it's all good. I kept away too long. I'm sorry."

Hill held Russell by the shoulders. "Man, I thought I'd seen a ghost. When you turned around I almost fell out of my chair."

"And when I saw you..." Russell shook his head and held his fist to his mouth to delay his tears.

"It's all good little brother." Hill patted him on the back.

"Grown men shouldn't cry," Russell remarked.

"Only if they are not real men without feelings. It's all good. I'm fighting my tears too." They hugged again. "So you're going by your middle name and using mom's maiden name now huh?"

"Yeah, needed a change," Russell said quietly.

"This is such a hallmark moment. Seems you two have a lot of catching up to do," I said, now standing between the two brothers.

"You're the best! Thanks baby." Hill gave me a kiss before I went to talk to my father. After five minutes, I went to mingle with the crowd and saw Trixie, Cassius, and Marcusetta. I was happy that they all came out to celebrate Hill's birthday. I had invited Ms. Benita, but she was spending the weekend in Atlantic City with Larry. On my way to the bar, I heard Angela's voice. I turned around to greet her. "Hey girl." I looked at my watch and noted the time.

"I know, I know, sorry I couldn't get here any sooner. Got a flat and had to wait for the tow truck. Whew, made it though. Girl, what'd I miss?" Angela asked.

I had to get used to calling Russell by his first name, Heath. But he insisted that I continue to call him Russell. He arranged to stay in town for a week at Hill's place. They needed some brotherly bonding time together. Russell had not spoken to his mother in years because she decided to stay with their father who had abused her physically for years when they were teenagers. He couldn't forgive the choice she made to stay with their father. Before he left town he had a heated argument with Hill and punches were thrown. But Hill chose to remain close to keep an eye on their mother. Hill told him that if he was around, their father would think twice before putting a finger on their mother and that's why he chose to stay.

After Russell left, the two brothers vowed to stay in touch and visit each other frequently. Russell told Hill to get on Facebook and sign up to follow him on Twitter as he travels around the country performing at various venues. He promised us VIP passes to any event we could make.

"I'm so glad you two found each other," I said, snuggling deeper into Hill's arms.

"It's the gods, the mighty ones, who made it happen and of course you. Wish I could've known Lia. Russell was smitten by her and torn up by her loss."

"He'll heal with time," I said.

"Yes, he will." Hill rolled onto his side and whispered to me, "I love you."

Did I hear right? Did he just use the L word?

I hesitated, but then finally said, "I love you too."

Hill gave me a peck on the cheek as he jumped out of bed and hopped into the shower. He began to whistle and as I nestled into bed, my cell phone rang. When I looked at the caller ID it was from a blocked number.

I answered. "Hello?"

"Deidre, don't hang up on me baby."

In the background, I heard an announcement: *"Now boarding our non-stop flight to Montego Bay, Jamaica."*

"Kyle? What the hell..."

AUTHOR'S NOTE

THIS IS NOT THE END! *Gotta Let It Go* is just the beginning of my Gotta "romantic suspense" series. Stay tuned for *Gotta Get It Back*, book two of this series which heats up again with Deidre, Hill, and Kyle. This time, they are caught up in the middle of a murder investigation involving a Baltimore City Circuit Court judge and are surrounded by deadly adversaries.

So, if you've enjoyed reading *Gotta Let It Go*, I'd really appreciate if you would spread the word by leaving a review on Amazon, Goodreads, other retail sites, or your blog.

For announcements about new releases, hop on over to my website and sign up for my newsletter mailing list at *www.authordeelawrence.com*. Your e-mail address will never be shared and you can unsubscribe at any time.

Thanks so much for your support, it means a lot to me!

Until next time…

Deliah Lawrence